BRANNIGAN

Despite being cleared of killing his best friend, Mark Henshall, Carl Brannigan was banished from home by his pa. Four years later, Brannigan returns. His welcome home is tempered by the knowledge that the Henshall family has brought ruin to his pa's cattle ranch. And amid more family shame, Carl tries to clear the Brannigan name and becomes a deputy marshal. But his hope of bringing the real culprits to justice means that he must face the threat of his past . . .

Books by Bill Williams
in the Linford Western Library:

ESCAPE FROM FORT ISAAC
KILLER BROTHERS
KILLINGS AT LETANA CREEK
SATAN'S GUN

BILL WILLIAMS

---◆---

BRANNIGAN

Complete and Unabridged

LINFORD
Leicester

First published in Great Britain in 2007 by
Robert Hale Limited
London

First Linford Edition
published 2008
by arrangement with
Robert Hale Limited
London

British Library CIP Data

Williams, Bill, *1940 –*
Brannigan.—Large print ed.—
Linford western library
1. Western stories
2. Large type books
I. Title
823.9′2 [F]

ISBN 978–1–84782–359–5

Published by
F. A. Thorpe (Publishing)
Anstey, Leicestershire

Set by Words & Graphics Ltd.
Anstey, Leicestershire
Printed and bound in Great Britain by
T. J. International Ltd., Padstow, Cornwall

This book is printed on acid-free paper

1

Carl Brannigan climbed into the saddle of the grey mare for the third time and cursed himself once again. He'd been at the entrance to his father's ranch for nearly an hour, trying to decide what to do. He didn't even know if his father, Henry, was still alive. It had been close to four years ago since Carl had been ordered off the land. Henry Brannigan's last words had been, 'Don't ever come back. You're a disgrace to the Brannigan name!'

Carl Brannigan had changed a lot and for the better, but wondered if he'd get a chance to explain that to his father. It hadn't mattered to Henry that the jury had cleared him. He'd been suspected of killing a man. Not a bad man, deserving what he got, but his best friend, Mark Henshall, after an argument over Isobel Clayman.

'Let's do this!' he murmured and urged the grey forward. So many boyhood memories came back as he approached the cabin which served as a ranch-house. They'd been happy days when Ma was alive and his cousins used to come over. Now there was just Carl, and maybe his father left in the immediate family.

Carl had never been one for taking much interest in the small ranch, but from what he could see the place looked much the same.

He'd just secured the grey's reins to the hitch rail when the door opened and he saw the rifle barrel pointing at him.

'What's your business here, mister?' the man holding the gun shouted as he stepped out on to the porch.

They studied each other for a moment.

Carl Brannigan was twenty-three years old; his brown hair was tucked under the black Stetson. The six-foot-two frame had filled out some, but

Henry Brannigan clearly had no trouble recognizing him.

Henry Brannigan had aged. The once upright figure was now stooped and the thin hair was mostly grey. The face was gaunt, but the voice was still strong when he lowered the rifle and said, 'Welcome home, boy.'

The words were those that Carl might have wished for, but could never have imagined being uttered by his father. Carl hadn't cried since the day his ma died during that fearsome winter six years ago, but the tears welled in his eyes as he climbed the steps to the porch and hugged his father.

'I'm sorry for bringing you so much grief, Pa, but I promise you that I've done a lot of growing up since I left.'

'And I'm sorry, son, for sending you away like I did. I've got some coffee brewing and I'll make you something to eat. You can tell me where that fine grey horse of yours has taken you.'

Carl nodded at the rifle in his father's hand and asked if there'd been any trouble.

'There's always the prospect of trouble, son, but I've reached nigh on fifty-five years of age by being careful. The old eyes aren't as good as they used to be and I've spent the last hour wondering who it was up by the gate. You were too far away for me to recognize the grey.'

Carl had planned to ride into town later, but he had so much catching up to do with his father and the time flew by. Henry had never been one for drinking in the saloon, but Carl discovered that he still made and drank a mean home-brewed beer.

'In case you're wondering, son, Isobel Clayman married a feller named John Cole about two years ago and they moved to a town near Mount Studmore. I'm not sure what it's called. Someone said that the Coles are a rich family who made their money back East.'

'I wouldn't have expected a girl like Isobel to have stayed single for long. I admit I've been curious about her, but

I hadn't planned to see her, especially if Mark's folks are still living out at the big place. I take it they are.'

Henry looked serious when he said, 'Only Vincent lives out at the ranch. Theodore died a couple of years back. He'd had a lot of problems with his heart and that's what killed him according to the doc. Within a couple of months of his death Martha moved to some city to live with her sister. Vincent always had more of a liking for liquor, gambling and fine suits than ranching and he sold off the herd last year and didn't replace it. Some folks say that the family was in debt even when Theodore was alive and Vincent will have to sell up soon because he's in trouble because of his gambling. Theodore and Vincent never spoke to me after your trial, but Martha used to wave to me when she was in town. She was always close to your ma and she's a lovely lady.'

'I'm sorry, Pa,' Carl said and took a gulp of the strong liquor.

'Don't be,' Henry said. 'I expect that they forgot that Mark was even wilder than you, and Isobel was your girl. Everyone knew that. Maybe if you hadn't both been out of your minds with the drink a lot of the time it might have been different. You were lucky that Joe Maple saw you leaving town when he was heading back to his store and testified that Mark was still alive after your brawling, otherwise you would have faced a hanging.'

'I don't suppose they ever found Mark's killer?' Carl asked and his father shook his head.

'What about your ranch, Pa? I didn't see any hired help on my ride in here.'

'The ranch is finished, son. I wasn't going to tell you, but you'll find out soon enough. After that business with Mark, Theodore put up some fencing and stopped my cattle from getting to the water or grazing on his land. So that was the end of it. I was approached by a lawyer a few months back saying that Vincent was prepared to give access to

6

the water if I paid him one thousand dollars a year. I decided that I would carry on with just a few animals and chickens, but maybe now that you're back it might be worth thinking about. I could just about afford it.'

Carl lifted the glass to his lips, but this time it was only a sip he took and then asked if Ned Dodds was still the marshal.

'He is, but I don't know for how long. Maple Town's changed, son. You'll see that. We have the railroad of course and the place is thriving, so it's not all bad. A lot of folks are unhappy with the marshal because he doesn't keep the cowhands in order and then there was the bank robbery just a month back and the death of little Lucy Morgan. You won't know the Morgan family. William Morgan and his brother Bryn took over the Maple's general store a couple of years ago. Theodore Henshall tried to get the council to change the name of the town to Henshall after Joe Maple had moved away. There aren't any

Maples left now except Zack Maple who the town was named after, but he's in the cemetery.'

Carl asked what had happened to the little girl.

'Little Lucy was shot by one of the gang during the bank robbery. The robbers haven't been caught and folks think that the marshal hasn't been doing enough to catch them.'

'Then I might have come home at the right time,' said Carl causing his father to give him a puzzled look.

'I was going to tell you later, Pa, that I hope to get a job as a deputy. It sounds as though the marshal could do with some help.'

Henry looked troubled and was shocked that his once wayward son could contemplate being a lawman. It would have been no less a surprise if he'd said that he had plans to become a preacher. Henry would have expected his son to have matured, perhaps even given some thought to taking himself a wife and settling down, but becoming a lawman was something different. He could imagine some folks in town sniggering if ever they heard about Carl's plans.

'I know you've never taken to ranching, son, but you can't be serious about becoming a deputy, surely not in Maple. Aren't you forgetting that you caused Marshal Dodds a heap of trouble? You and Mark Henshall must have spent more nights in his cells than anyone else in town.'

'That was a long time ago, Pa, and I've told you that I've changed. For most of the last year I worked as a deputy in Bugle Falls and I've got a letter in my saddle-bag from the marshal there. You know — a sort of reference. I'll show it to Marshal Dodds and I'm sure he'll forget all those things Mark and me got up to. Anyway it was mostly for brawling and we didn't always start the trouble.'

Henry frowned, got up from his seat and said, 'I'm not sure I like the idea of you being a lawman, son. Not in Maple or anywhere else for that matter. We'll talk some more in the morning. There's something I need to tell you about the bank robbery, but it'll wait. I'm going to check on the horses. You'll find some dry blankets in your old room. Sleep well, son.'

Carl bade his father goodnight, gulped back the remaining liquor from the glass and headed to the bedroom. Both men seemed at ease with the world; Carl could never have guessed what awaited them.

2

Marshal Ned Dodds wasn't happy with the accusations being flung at him by the deputation from the town council and hoped his promise that things would get better soon would satisfy them.

'We don't want promises, Marshal — we want action,' said Mayor Bradley Jefferson, after removing the cigar from his mouth.

'And so do I, sir. More than you can imagine, but I think you're forgetting just how big Maple has become. A town this size is always going to attract those looking for trouble.'

'And what about the bank robbery?' snapped Bryn Morgan. 'It's been over a month now and you haven't made a single arrest. Frankly, that's just not good enough.'

Marshal Dodds's broad frame fidgeted in his seat. He was forty-eight years old with dark brown eyes that would out-stare most men and his black hair was thick and unruly. His face showed few signs of the stress caused by being a lawman for over twenty years; now he was trying to control his anger when he replied: 'I appreciate you being upset, Mr Morgan, with you being that poor little girl's uncle. Her loss must be felt by you all. The fact is that I need the extra help that I've asked for and I'm still waiting for the town council to approve the finance.'

Bryn Morgan was a tall, slim built man of forty-four years, being two years younger than his brother, William. His normally smiling face belied that he was a ruthless businessman. He was usually calm and good natured, except like now when he was angry. 'What you need, Marshal, is some determination to catch the killer. I'm not interested in cowboys letting off steam. We can tolerate that because they bring business into the town. What we can't accept is a child being gunned down in the street.'

'Then give me the finance so I can take on two experienced men, not some young kids who fancy their chances with a gun. I think you folks forget what a difference the railroad and cattle drives have made to this town. You all want the business, but don't want to pay for the consequences they bring. Times have changed, and you can't have law and order without paying for it and that includes trying to bring in those bank robbers to face justice.'

'The marshal's right,' said Mayor Jefferson, and looked as though he was deliberating before he continued, 'I tell you what I'll do, Marshal. I'll fund a new deputy for the next six months while the town council gets its finances sorted out.'

Dodds relaxed a little, grateful that the offer had taken the heat out of the meeting. 'That's much appreciated, Mr Mayor. It will help, but I'll still need another one, so you might bear that in mind when the council does its review.'

'Point noted, Marshal. Now I think

we'll leave you to get on with your work. Good day to you.'

There were mumbled words of encouragement from the others and they followed the mayor out of the office.

Dodds banged his fist on the desk once he was alone and roared, 'Damn greedy, that's what they are!'

Dodds had to do some thinking about where he was going to find a suitable deputy for the same rate they paid WJ, his current deputy, which was a miserly ten dollars. WJ was willing enough, but he wasn't cut out to be a lawman. Perhaps, Dodds wondered, it was time to pack it all in and get on with his plans for the future, even though he liked the town. The way things were going he might end up with a bullet in him, and for what! If the town council couldn't be bothered to face up to the problems, then why should he take it in the neck? There were other towns that respected a good marshal with his experience and paid

14

accordingly. It was a pity the members of the town council didn't join him on his rounds once in a while, especially when the cattle drives came into town. Then they would see what he had to put up with.

3

Carl forced his eyes open and it took a while for it to sink in that his pain was over. He was home with his Pa and ready to start a new life. Although Pa hadn't been keen about the idea of him becoming a lawman, he might change his mind when he'd read the glowing reference from Marshal Bob Took whom he'd worked for in Bugle Falls in south Nevada. Bugle Falls might be one of the smallest towns in the territory, but it was also one of the roughest. Carl had discovered that the miners who came into town from the hills could be as mean as hell. And even some of the town folks could be a heap of trouble and he'd ended up killing one of them in the line of duty.

Maybe his father had hoped he would help out at the ranch and that's why he appeared none too pleased. He had warned Carl that Marshal Dodds and the town council might not be too eager to employ a man who had spent more time than most in the cells. Carl had often wondered why he had been so bad. He wasn't one for making excuses, except that he was young at the time and he didn't handle liquor very well, but it was mainly that he couldn't walk away from trouble.

Carl tested the heat of the coffee pot and decided that his father must have gone about his chores early. He settled for the lukewarm liquid and made his way out into the morning sun, stopping by the water butt to swill the sleep from his eyes and then lit up a cigar as he made his way to the barn.

He stopped to watch the chickens scurrying about the yard and pondered on the lonely life that his father must lead. Then his eyes scanned the view of the rolling green meadows that contrasted with the blue of the unblemished sky. The terrain was mostly flat apart from an expanse to the west that had a range of small hills that had once made his father consider grazing sheep there. He was saddened to see broken fencing around the corral that once contained the stallion that had sired his present horse. The fence couldn't have deteriorated naturally in the time he'd been away so perhaps it had been used for firewood. He intended to ask if there were any urgent jobs that he could help with before he pursued his own plans. Wherever he settled, Carl intended to make sure that he made frequent visits back here and not neglect his father.

★　★　★

Maybe it was the dim light in the barn that caused the delay before he realized what confronted him; then the horror registered and he screamed out, 'No!'

Carl frantically climbed up on to the small cart that his father must have jumped from after he'd tied the rope around his neck. Carl leapt down when he realized that his outstretched hand

18

couldn't reach his father. He scanned the barn looking for a knife or tool and grabbed a small scythe and then positioned the cart beneath the dangling figure. He clambered on to the cart and held the rope with one hand and used the scythe to hack through it; then he lowered his father on to the straw that covered the floor of the cart.

He had seen enough dead men to know that the blueness and cold skin of his father meant that he was beyond help, but it didn't stop him from sobbing, 'Don't die, Pa, not now. Please don't die.'

He cradled the man he'd thought he'd hated for a short time, but knew he'd always loved. He finally stopped pleading for his father not to die and then repeated over and over, 'Why, Pa!' and then he noticed something that might explain what had happened. In his rush to release his father from the rope he hadn't seen the small white bag displaying the words 'Maple Bank'.

Carl removed his arm from beneath

his father's head which he rested back on to the straw and then undid the string on the bag and pulled out the dollar bills. He guessed there must have been about a thousand dollars. His thoughts flashed back to last night. Pa had said that he had the thousand dollars to pay Vincent Henshall for water access and grazing rights. His parting words were that he had something to tell him about the bank robbery. He'd seen his father's eyes mist up when he mentioned the little girl who'd been shot. He looked down at his father in disbelief. He just couldn't accept the idea that his father could have taken part in a bank robbery. But here he was looking at the evidence. And then he was struck by the thought that his father would be alive if he hadn't come home. Maybe it was the guilt of the little girl's death or the shame it would bring on his son if he was found out. Perhaps he'd even considered that Carl himself might uncover his involvement if he became a deputy marshal. Carl hugged his father again and sobbed as he said, 'You old fool!'

He covered the body in preparation for taking it into town later and then went back into the house. None of this made sense. There had to be an explanation. Perhaps the thousand dollars he mentioned last night was hidden somewhere in the cabin. His father had never believed in using banks so if he had money it must be in the house. Carl searched every possible place that the money could have been hidden, not because he wanted it, but to prove that his father hadn't been referring to stolen money to use to pay Vincent Henshall. He found a few hundred dollars under the heavy wooden dresser as well as a medal that he knew had been awarded to his Grandpa Brannigan for fighting in a war in the old country, which was England.

Carl finally decided that even if he'd found a large amount of money in the

21

house that wasn't stolen money it still wouldn't prove his pa's innocence. The fact was that his father would have needed a lot more money because he would have had to restock the herd. There would have been no point in obtaining water and grazing rights unless he had a sizeable herd. There was still a chance that more of his father's own money could have been hidden in the barn or one of the outbuildings and he planned to search those when he came back from arranging the funeral.

He sat in his father's chair and gazed around the room and went over some of the things that had been said last night. In a moment of melancholy he questioned whether his father had done it to pay him back. Perhaps blaming him in some way for what he had done. Carl was now thinking that his father couldn't have done it to spare him the shame if his secret got out because that's what he would face now, unless he lied about how his father died. But what about the marks on his neck! How would he explain those away? He might even get blamed for strangling his own pa because folks would think that there had been bad feeling between them right to the end. Maybe his father had intended for Carl to bury him secretly somewhere on his own land and keep the money.

Carl pushed his rambling thoughts from his mind. Perhaps Pa had lost his way and his thinking had been muddled, but Carl knew that the old pa would have wanted him to come clean and that's what he intended to do. He would return the money to the marshal and tell him the truth. He would face the consequence and hope his revelation might help catch the other robbers and comfort the little girl's family in their grief.

Carl felt cheated because he had been robbed of the happier times he'd planned with his Pa. After yesterday's welcome he was looking forward to making amends for the way he had messed up. He'd sometimes thought that perhaps if Pa had been less strict then he might not have been so rebellious. Pa had been brought up in hard times when the toil of work sapped a man's energy and left little time for pleasure and maybe he should have taken into account that times had changed, but Carl wasn't blaming him for any of his own shortcomings. The truth was that Carl had come under the influence of the Henshalls who lived in a different world to ordinary folk and pleasure-seeking was a large part of their lives. It was as though they lived as if there was no tomorrow.

4

It was close to noon when Carl pulled on the reins of the sturdy black gelding and brought the cart to a halt midway down Main Street outside the premises of Stanley Beaumont, the town's undertaker. He hoped no one went nosing under the covers on the cart while he went inside because if they did they would discover the body.

Mr Beaumont raised his small wiry body off his seat and came from behind his desk. 'How can we help you, young sir?' was his greeting, which signalled to Carl that the thin faced man dressed from head to toe in black, hadn't recognized him. The last time they'd spoken was at his ma's funeral six years ago.

Carl introduced himself and explained that he'd come to arrange a funeral for his father whose body was on the cart outside.

Mr Beaumont tucked in his chin and peered over his gold rimmed spectacles. 'Please accept my sincere condolences and my apologies for not recognizing you. If you'll excuse me I'll arrange for one of my assistants to bring your father around the back. Please take a seat and I'll be with you presently.'

Mr Beaumont took less than hour to arrange for Henry to be buried at 11 o'clock in the morning. He confirmed that a space had been reserved next to where Martha Brannigan had been laid to rest. Carl hadn't wanted to go into the details of his father's death before he'd reported it to Marshal Dodds, but he found himself partly drawn into it when Beaumont expressed his surprise that only Carl would be attending the burial service.

'The fact is, Mr Beaumont, my pa took his own life and there will be lots of speculation why he did it. My guess is that very few folks will want to pay their respects once the news gets out. When I leave here I'm heading for the marshal's office to report Pa's death and then folks will have to think what they want. I'm sorry I can't tell you more, but I think you'll understand.'

Stanley Beaumont assured Carl that Henry Brannigan would be buried with dignity and God's forgiveness whatever reasons he'd had for taking his own life.

Beaumont's assistant had brought the empty cart around the front and Carl decided to walk the short distance up Main Street to the marshal's office. Mr Beaumont had been helpful and tactful given the circumstances, but Carl wasn't expecting the marshal and other folks to be the same. He was relieved when he reached the marshal's office without meeting anyone who might have remembered him. The town had a feeling of prosperity and an extra saloon by the name of Margo's Place. He quickly glanced away when he saw the large sign displaying the name *Morgan Brothers* above the general store that was down the street. His father had told him that the Morgans were good folks, but he didn't expect anything but hostility from them.

As he stepped on the sidewalk the door opened and he was greeted by a voice he recognized. 'Well I'll be damned! It's Carl Brannigan.' Deputy Warwick J Everett's face broke into a broad smile.

'Howdy, WJ. I'd never have had you down as a lawman. Is the marshal in?' Carl asked, trying to sound cheerful and not show his grief. He remembered that WJ had no living family and now he was in the same position.

'He is, but he's in an ugly mood. I'm just off to do my rounds otherwise I'd go back in with you to see his reaction. You aren't exactly his favourite person, but it would be true to say that things haven't been any quieter while you've been away. I'll catch up with you later and you can tell me what you've been up to and what life was like in prison.' WJ added, 'I'm only kidding,' before Carl told him that he hadn't been to prison.

Carl gave a weak smile as he watched the lanky deputy head across the street. They hadn't exactly been buddies in the old days, but he'd always liked WJ who had an easygoing nature. He'd once told Carl that the name Warwick was a place in England where his father's family came from, but he preferred to be called WJ.

Carl took a deep breath and entered the marshal's office, determined to get through what was going to be a difficult reunion.

'This is all I need,' Marshall Dodds groaned when he looked up from his paperwork.

'You needn't worry about me, Marshal. I'm not going to bring you any trouble. That was a long time ago.'

'I'm not worried, Brannigan, and you should remember that you're not a high spirited kid anymore and you won't get off lightly if you step out of line.'

Marshal Dodds told Carl that he would be spending time in prison if he did. The new circuit judge was strict and he wouldn't get away with brawling like he used to. The marshal was about to lay down the law some more when Carl interrupted him and said, 'I've come to report that my pa's dead.'

'Well I'm sorry to hear that, Brannigan. I was only talking to him a couple of days ago. I remember him being a bit edgy. How did it happen?'

Carl was surprised that the marshal hadn't eyed him with suspicion or even asked if he'd been involved.

'He went and hung himself from a beam in the barn. I only got home yesterday and things were fine between us. Not a bad word crossed his lips and then I found him this morning.'

'There's no point in denying that you're not very popular around here, Brannigan, and I'm not just talking about Mark Henshall's family, but your pa was well liked.'

Carl undid the saddle-bag that he'd brought with him and removed the Maple Bank bag that he'd found in the barn and placed it on the desk.

'There are a few things that you need to know, Marshal.'

When Carl had finished telling him where he'd found the money and about his father's plans to tell him something about the robbery, the marshal took a deep sigh.

'It just doesn't make sense, Brannigan. I can't see your pa ever being involved in a minor misdemeanour, let alone a bank raid.' The marshal looked thoughtful as he stared at the dollar bills that Carl had taken from the bag and then added: 'But there doesn't seem to be any other explanation and I sense that even you have accepted that he must have been connected with the robbery.'

Carl nodded his head and said, 'He had to have been, but it's hard to imagine him pulling a gun on someone. He taught me to handle a pistol, but he never wore one when he came into town.'

'If your pa was involved then he might have been the man on the roof who was covering the other two who did the actual robbery, because he didn't fit the description of either of them. It was the man on the roof who shot a young girl named Lucy Morgan, but I'm sure that whoever killed her didn't mean to.'

Carl grimaced at the thought of the anguish it must have caused his pa and made him take his own life to ease the pain.

'I admire your guts for coming here, Brannigan, but I'm going to have to break the news to the town council. I could hold off telling them until your pa has been buried if you want me to.'

Carl declined the marshal's offer and explained that the funeral was tomorrow. It wouldn't be fair if folks attended and then found out later what his father had done.

Before Carl left he told the marshal about his plans to become a deputy, explaining about his experience and his letter from Marshal Took back in Bugle Falls.

'I can see you've changed, Brannigan, and I know you can handle yourself. It so happens that I urgently need some help. I would be prepared to take you on trial, but I'm afraid there might be a lot of opposition from some folks on the town council when they hear what your pa did and then there's your old reputation to consider. You might be better starting a new life in another town. Perhaps it might be best if you went back to Bugle Falls, but I'll still put your name forward and see what the council have to say. Some of the council are newcomers to the town and so they won't be prejudiced against you. It might help if you drop by with that reference from Bugle Falls.'

Carl had strong reasons for not wanting to return to Bugle Falls, but he wasn't about to share them with the marshal, nor was he thinking of running away from the town where he'd been born, at least not until he'd thought things through. He told the marshal that he would bring the letter in tomorrow and then added, 'I might just stay around and try and find out why Pa would have got involved in a robbery. Perhaps you can help me there, Marshal. Did you ever see him mixing with anyone who might be the sort to commit a robbery?'

Dodds rubbed his chin before he replied, 'I didn't see a lot of him and he never used the saloons. So, I can't help you there. I'm probably as shocked as you are because he always seemed as straight as they come. He was an old fashioned pillar of the community, I suppose.'

'Someone must have seen him with the others,' said Carl. 'They would have been together while they were planning the robbery. I'll ask around and if I find anything useful I'll pass it on to you.'

The marshal looked serious when he said, 'I'd want to do the same in your situation, Brannigan, but I wouldn't be happy if you started hassling folks or if you took the law into your own hands. I think its best if you leave the investigation to me. I still have a few ideas of my own and they may try to rob somewhere else and get caught. They may even have another go at the Maple Bank. Lightning does strike twice when it comes to robberies. You must be prepared to get the cold shoulder from people, even old friends of your pa. It might have been different if it was just a simple robbery, but folks will find it hard to forgive because of that little girl. I'm afraid you may have been left a terrible cross to bear.'

'I appreciate what you're saying, Marshal, but I don't plan to just accept this. I won't hold out much hope of becoming your deputy and I can understand why it might not be possible. I'm sure I would have learned a lot from you.'

'Never say never, Brannigan, but I think you know the score. If you do stay around perhaps we can have a chin-wag sometime about your time in Bugle Falls.'

'Sure,' was all Carl replied and bid the marshal farewell and headed for Doc Aubrey's small surgery which was down the street.

Doc Aubrey wasn't exactly in the best of health, mainly on account of being just about the biggest man Carl had ever seen. He was in his late fifties, with a heavy-jowled face that wobbled when he laughed, which was quite often. But when Carl related what had happened the doc sighed heavily and looked troubled.

'I'm truly sorry, young Carl, but I've been around long enough not to be shocked like you and other folks will be. This town is becoming more and more prosperous for some, but for others it's become hard to make a living. It might pain you to know that your pa was struggling. Oh, he was never going to starve, but he seemed to have lost his purpose. The Henshalls did the dirty on him by denying his cattle access like they'd done for all those years when things were friendly between your families. I told him to take them to the courts, but he said it would be too expensive.'

Carl asked the doc if he'd seen his father with anyone suspicious who might have been a member of the gang. The doc just shook his head and then added, 'Of course it's possible that the other two might be just as unlikely robbers as your pa was. Men can be driven to do strange things when they're desperate. If you want to find the robbers you might want to look towards some of your pa's old friends and not expect them to be what you might think are typical types, if that makes any sense.'

Despite his troubles Carl managed a smile and suggested that the doc would have made a good marshal and he intended to take what he had said very seriously. Before he left, the doc asked about the funeral and promised to be there if nothing urgent came up. Carl was thinking that perhaps his father's partners in crime might also attend. He would study the gathering, if there was one, in case their behaviour might give him cause to suspect them. Marshal Took had taught him to look out for what he called body language which often revealed someone's intent. He had used it to good effect when trying to spot a troublemaker and especially when a man was about to go for his gun. Carl had been advised that it was best to look at the eyes if the man was close enough and not at his gun-hand which was what most folks made the mistake of doing.

5

Carl's prediction about there not being many folks at the funeral turned out to be correct and it was only attended by Mrs Logan the retired schoolteacher, who had been his Ma's best friend and Doc Aubrey. So he could forget about discovering if some of Pa's friends might have been involved in the robbery, but perhaps they might make a secret visit to the graveside when the funeral was over.

He would find out later that it was only the intervention of the marshal that had stopped some folks from venting their anger on the funeral procession as it had passed along Main Street.

Mrs Logan was frail and he held her arm during the short walk to the graveside.

Reverend Black was away on some

church business so Mr Beaumont conducted the short service, and as he'd promised, Henry Brannigan was buried with dignity.

After the funeral Carl escorted Mrs Logan back to the small buggy that her granddaughter had brought her in and she kissed him on the cheek and said, 'Young Carl, folks who say that your pa did that terrible thing just didn't know him. I don't care what the evidence was, he didn't do it.'

Carl wished he could have shown the same loyalty and faith towards his father as the sweet old lady, but life was hard and it had already been mentioned to him that it could cause decent men to do desperate things.

Carl waved off Mrs Logan and Doc Aubrey, thanked Mr Beaumont for his help and then he returned to the graves of his folks and sat contemplating what he should do. From his vantage point he would be able to see if any of his father's missing friends turned up.

* ★ ★

By the time he was preparing to leave
the cemetery he had decided that he
would board up the ranch and sell the
livestock before moving on to the next
town and pursue his plans to become
a deputy. The marshal had made it
clear that he wasn't happy with the
idea of Carl doing his own investigation into the robbery so he would
leave it to him, at least for now. Carl
intended to return in a few months'
time and hope that things would have
settled down and if he still had
Marshal Dodds' support he would try
again to become one of his deputies.
Mrs Logan's praise for his father had
worried him and he wondered if there
was any possibility that she was right.
If he was a deputy at Maple he would
be well placed to look into the robbery
and see how his father became
involved with the robbers.

He had just walked away from the
graves when he saw the two figures

approaching. One was a pretty girl with curly auburn hair that rested on her shoulders and when she came closer he saw the large dark brown eyes before she lowered them. He wondered if she might be someone he knew when she was a girl and had blossomed into this beautiful woman. He decided that she wasn't, and that she must have moved here since he'd left. The man with her was no stranger. It was Vincent Henshall, Mark's brother. Vincent hadn't changed much except his face had the flushed look of someone who consumed too much liquor or rich food. He had always been a smart dresser and he was wearing an expensive looking dark green suit with matching Stetson and highly polished boots. He was taller than most men and still slim. He had a long nose, dark greyish eyes and thin black moustache. Some folks would have called him a charmer and maybe a lady's man. He'd always had a keen interest in horses and been more scholarly and gentlemanly than his wild brother, Mark.

'That's him, Shelley, the man I was telling you about. That's Carl Brannigan, my brother's murderer and the son of the man who killed your precious little sister. He belongs in a bygone age of wild primitives.'

'I'm sorry for your grief, miss,' Carl said and then his face looked mean as he faced her companion. 'I've just buried my pa, Vincent, and this is not the place for hollering like you are. If you've something to say to me then I'll be in one of the saloons for the next hour.'

Carl turned and walked away. He could tell that Shelley Morgan was embarrassed and upset and he was eager not to make her feel worse and so he ignored Vincent when he called after him.

'You haven't changed, Brannigan. You still think you can solve everything with your fists or gun. If you had any decency then you would leave and never set foot in this town again.'

Carl hadn't planned to call in at the saloon, but now he felt he had to, even though he doubted if Vincent would come looking for him.

Most of the hitch rails outside the Toledo Saloon had horses tethered to them and Carl was tempted to ride on. Then the memory of having his first drink in there with his father came to him and he thought it would be fitting to go in and make a silent toast.

He recognized a few faces as he made his way to the bar and he knew from the hostility in their expressions that the news about his father had spread. They might have been recalling what had happened to Mark, but he doubted it because folks had been friendly enough towards him before he'd left not long after the trial.

'It just isn't proper burying killers amongst decent folks,' called out a man at the card table. Carl turned to face him, his hand moving close to his gun. All of the men at the card table froze with fear.

Carl moved towards the man and shouted, 'You've got a big mouth, mister. Why don't we go out into the street and you can tell me what's bothering you?'

'Take no notice of him, Carl,' said the voice behind him. It was WJ who then added, 'You're right, Carl, about Monkton having a big mouth.'

'I was only saying what most folks feel,' said Bob Monkton as he gathered his money from the table and made a hasty retreat from the saloon, grateful that Deputy Everett had intervened. He didn't know Carl Brannigan, but he'd heard about his reputation and he looked as mean as hell.

'Thanks, WJ,' said Carl. He moved his hand away from his gun and relaxed a little. 'I would probably have beaten hell out of that feller and ended up across the street in one of your cells and that would have put an end to my plans.'

WJ looked uneasy and said, 'Marshal Dodds mentioned about you wanting to be a deputy, but I've got some bad news. I was there when he suggested it to the mayor. He pushed really hard to get you hired, but the mayor said something about it not being appropriate. The marshal told me I was to tell you the news if I saw you. He mentioned something about not bothering to bring in a reference.'

'To be honest, WJ, I'm not surprised. Anyway, let me buy you a beer.'

Carl's call to the barman for two beers was followed by another voice from along the bar. It was Dale Sommers who ran the town's livery. 'No offence, Brannigan, but you aren't welcome here. I don't agree with what Monkton said about your pa and the cemetery, but you being around reminds us of what happened to the girl.'

Carl had already decided that he wasn't going to leave before he'd had his drink. Maybe he should forget about being a lawman and sort out these narrow minded people who wanted to have a go at him.

'I can understand the girl's family being heartbroken and I'm truly sorry about that, but I aim to have me a drink. I've just buried my Pa and I don't want any trouble, but I ain't going to be picked on. Now if you know what's good for you then you'll leave me be.'

The barman stopped pouring the beer, undecided what to do. WJ looked uneasy and was relieved when Sommers looked away and continued drinking his beer.

'Let's go over to Margo's Place, Carl. You won't have any trouble there,' suggested WJ.

'I just want one beer, WJ. It's important to me and you have my word that I won't cause any trouble.'

'What's keeping those beers, barman?' WJ called out, after he'd decided that Carl would honour his promise not to start any trouble.

When the beer arrived Carl raised his glass in a mock toast to his father and then drank the contents without pausing. His eyes were moist when he thanked WJ and told him he was heading for Margo's and wanted to be on his own for a while, but he would be heading home soon.

'Stay cool, buddy,' said WJ as he shook Carl's hand and then watched him walk out of the saloon.

★　★　★

Margo's Place was brightly decorated compared to the Toledo Saloon and there seemed to be as many saloon girls as there were customers. The blonde-haired girl sat at the bar winked at him, but didn't speak when he gave her a blank look. He might not be interested, but it hadn't stopped him noticing her ample breasts. She must have been in her mid thirties, but he'd enjoyed some of his best times with older women.

Carl was still musing about older women when a heavily-made-up lady appeared behind the bar and told the barman that Carl's first drink was on the house. She must have been close to fifty years of age, but from what he could see of her body she was in good shape. The makeup didn't hide all of the heavy lines on her face, and the thick lipstick made her look hideous. She introduced herself as Margo, but he withheld his own name and she left him to his drink and circulated amongst the other customers.

The beer tasted good and he was soon forgetting his plans to head home. The atmosphere was lively as the bar began to fill up and it helped take his mind off things. His mood changed when Margo approached him and said, 'You're the one who buried his pa today, aren't you?' He was preparing for being asked to leave when she said, 'I'm sorry for your grief, cowboy.' Now he was thinking that she was a nice lady and then she added, 'I expect you'd like some company upstairs. Molly over there seems to have taken a shine to you.'

So perhaps she wasn't kind after all and just a business woman!

'Maybe later,' he said. 'Thanks for your sympathy.'

She smiled at him and walked away. It was a warm smile and he felt comfortable again and ordered another beer.

Carl was about to approach Molly when he saw her leading a drunken cowboy upstairs. The man was old enough to be her pa and although there were lots of other girls for Carl to choose from, seeing the man with Molly put him off and he decided to head for home.

He got another smile from Margo and he waved to her on his way to the door, but his path was blocked when a man headbutted a young kid and sent him sprawling in front of Carl. He had noticed the kid earlier and had been amused by his antics. Carl had decided that it might have been the kid's first time in a saloon and he wasn't used to drinking liquor.

The bearded man stood over the kid

whose broken nose was spilling blood on to the floor.

'I told you to stop gawping at my woman, you horny little runt,' said the man who then kicked the kid in the side. He was about to deliver a second kick when Carl pushed him aside and said, 'Leave the kid, mister. I'm sure he didn't mean any offence. He's just had too much to drink.'

The man glowered at Carl and looked him up and down, clearly assessing him. He must have decided that he could take Carl on and said, 'I can't abide people who stick their nose into other people's business.'

The bully lunged forwards, making it easy for Carl to butt him on a nose that had obviously been broken before. The sound of cracking bone was easily heard above the saloon's background noise. Carl pushed him as he fell to stop him falling on the kid and then he kicked him as he lay on the floor. He was about to kick him for a second time when he heard a gun being cocked.

'Hold it right there, Brannigan.' It was the voice of Marshal Dodds who was standing near the saloon door and was pointing his gun at Carl. WJ was with him.

'A leopard never changes its spots. Take him over the street, WJ and lock him up.'

WJ had pulled out his gun and he looked awkward when he ordered Carl to unbuckle his gunbelt and drop it to the floor.

'It wasn't his fault, Marshal,' pleaded Margo who didn't seem upset by the amount of blood on the floor. She had probably seen much worse in her time.

'It never is, sweetheart. Trouble just follows him,' Dodds said sarcastically and then ordered someone to go and get the doc.

'Now move, Brannigan. I think you know the way,' the marshal ordered.

Carl made the trip to the cells without any protest. He didn't want to cause WJ any grief, nor the marshal for that matter. He was beginning to feel the effects of the drink so he was happy to sleep it off in the cells and it would avoid having to spend a night on his own at the end of this sad day.

6

Carl awoke several times during the night, mostly because the cowboy who'd been thrown into his cell shortly after he'd gone to sleep, was either puking or snoring. The two men in the adjoining cell had started fighting and had been tied up by WJ, but they had continued cursing and threatening each other.

It was close to ten o'clock when Carl decided that he wasn't going to get any more sleep. His mouth was parched and his head throbbed. He didn't often suffer with the drink, but then again he had gulped down more than usual.

'Are you the feller who laid out big Johno?' asked the little guy who had just raised himself off the bed.

'I don't know anyone called Johno. Who is he?' asked Carl.

'Everyone knows Johno. He's a

bare-knuckle fighter. They say he was unbeaten until last night. I expect he'll want a rematch.'

Carl was more interested in getting something to take the dryness from his throat and rattled the bars of the cell. He was also eager to get away from the smell of the puke that was on the floor near his cell mate's bed.

He had hoped that WJ might have appeared, but it was the marshal and he looked grim faced. 'I was just coming to get you, Brannigan. We have important business to discuss. There have been some serious developments on account of what you did last night.'

'Holy shit!' said the little fellow, 'You must have killed Johno. I guess there won't be any rematch after all.'

Carl felt sick. He remembered the sound of the cracking bone, and the thud when the man's head hit the bar room floor.

'Hey, Marshal. Was it really Johno that this feller laid out in Margo's last night? He's one hell of a fighter is Johno.'

'It was, but Johno's fighting days are over,' the marshal replied.

'Jesus! You did kill him. You've earned yourself a place in folklore, mister, and so have I. I spent the night in a cell with the man who killed a legend without using a weapon.'

'Shut up, mouthy, or I'll turn you out without even a mug of coffee,' snapped Marshal Dodds.

Carl was numbed by the thought that his life would once again be in the hands of a jury. He followed the marshal out into the main office and the two men nodded to him. One was WJ, but he didn't know the older man who had a square jaw and bushy eyebrows and was kitted out in a black suit that reminded him of Mr Beaumont. He couldn't be an undertaker. Perhaps he was a judge.

'Brannigan, this is Mr Jefferson and he's here on official business.'

Carl was puzzled when Jefferson offered him his large hand and said that he was pleased to meet him. There was only one explanation. Johno wasn't dead and this was his manager and he wanted Carl to become a bare-knuckle fighter in place of Johno. Carl was remembering the scarred face of the bully. He wasn't a vain man but he didn't fancy having his features changed either, not to mention parting with his teeth. He reminded himself that this was no time for joking, although something was amusing WJ as he appeared to be struggling to stop himself from grinning.

'Brannigan, Mr Jefferson is the mayor and he's ordered me to give you the vacant deputy's job that you wanted. That's if you're still interested now you know how some folks feel about your pa.'

'I'm still interested,' said a surprised Carl and then added, 'I didn't start that trouble last night.'

'We know, and that's why the mayor is here,' said the marshal.

Mayor Jefferson coughed and then explained, 'It was my son, Daniel who you saved from a beating and perhaps worse. I figured that a man who would put himself at risk to save someone must be public spirited. And you can't be blamed for whatever your father might or might not have done. So you'll take the job then?'

'I will, sir, and thank you,' replied a shocked Carl.

'It's me who needs to do the thanking. I'll promise you one thing, Deputy, and that is you will not be seeing my son in a saloon for a very long time. And when the time comes for him to venture back in one, his busted nose will be a permanent reminder to make sure that he always keeps his wits about him.'

Everyone laughed and the mayor shook Carl's hand once more and said he would leave the marshal to swear him in.

When Carl approached the cell a short time later he was carrying a mug of coffee. His former cell mate's mouth dropped open when he saw the badge pinned to Carl's shirt. Maybe he was thinking this was a crazy town if a man was made a deputy after they had killed someone. He would be even more puzzled later when he saw a punch drunk Johno riding out of town, probably never to fight again judging by the vacant look on his face.

Carl had some breakfast with WJ and headed home, intending to return the following day and do his first stint as Deputy Marshal of Maple Town.

As he rode the three mile journey to what was now his ranch he marvelled at the terrain. It was mostly flat and although not spectacular it had a special beauty of its own, particularly where the trail ran beside the banks of the River Tundry which was occasionally shielded by magnificent pine trees. As he got closer to home the grass became lusher alongside the fencing that separated his ranch from the Henshalls'. He was reminded that this was why his pa and Theodore Henshall had settled here. Carl wasn't sure what he would do with the ranch, but he didn't intend to make a hasty decision. After all, it was the only home that he'd known and it was full of memories. The ranch house needed some repair work and the corral fence replacing, but he would enjoy restoring it to its former condition when he was off duty. He may not have been much of a cattleman, but his pa had taught some other skills, including carpentry. He also intended to keep the livestock and perhaps build it up, and then maybe in time he could take on some hired help. Perhaps he could be both a lawman and a rancher. Why not, he was thinking, as he approached the short trail that led to what had been his home. He pulled on the reins, shocked at the sight of the burnt out cabin and the nearby barn that had suffered the same fate. The sheds that had housed the animals and chickens had been reduced to a mound of ashes. Whoever had done this had taken their meanness and revenge out on the livestock. They must have all perished because he couldn't see any evidence that they had been released or escaped.

Carl headed back into town an hour later and his saddlebag contained the single item that he'd found amongst the ashes. It was a photograph of his ma and pa. It was scorched, but his folks were visible and it was nothing short of a miracle that it had somehow survived the blaze.

Carl climbed the steps to the marshal's office still shocked and wondering who had caused such devastation to his ranch. It might have been the mouthy feller in the saloon who'd had a go at him, but he doubted it. He decided that the person at the top of his list had to be Vincent Henshall, but proving it would be difficult.

7

Carl struggled to hide his nervousness when he pushed open the swing doors of the Toledo Saloon. He'd visited it for the first time as a lawman with Marshal Dodds last night, but now he was on his own. He was 'going solo' as the marshal had put it, and told him that he would only be across the street if he needed help. So far Carl was enjoying working for the marshal, knowing that he would learn a lot from the experienced lawman. Dodds could be ruthless with troublemakers, but he had a reputation for being fair and he was respected by the local men who knew that although he could be friendly he wasn't a man to take liberties with. The blonde-haired saloon girl he'd heard someone call Lily last night gave him a smile. She took a long puff on her freshly lit cigarette and then exhaled the smoke through her nostrils. The bar was only half full and by the time he'd reached it, the bald headed barman with the sweaty face and large belly had poured him a beer.

Carl raised his hand to signal that he didn't want the drink that was pushed towards him and said, 'No thanks.'

'You'll be wasting the marshal's money if you don't accept it because he's already paid for it and the boss doesn't allow me to issue refunds.'

Carl picked up the glass of frothy beer and took a large gulp, wondering if Dodds had figured he would need it to steady his nerves. Still it was a thoughtful gesture by the marshal and one he would remember if ever he became a marshal and had a young deputy under his wing. A quick glance around the bar didn't reveal anyone he knew, but his relief was short-lived when he looked towards the swing doors and recognized the Collins brothers. Ike Collins was Carl's age and he was still skinny and his skin was the same deathly white. His eyes appeared as narrow slits, and he rarely smiled and when he did it was usually a snigger. He was still wearing his favourite black outfit and carried a pair of Smith & Wesson's. Ike was the spitting image of his late father, Bandy Collins, who had been hung for shooting a man because he wouldn't buy his horse so he could carry on gambling. The other Collins was Arnie who was a couple of years younger and about as different to Ike as you could get. He was much shorter than Ike and his flabby red face seemed to sport a permanent grin. He was wearing a denim suit and the single holstered gunbelt had slipped out of position. Carl was thinking that it wouldn't be much use if he had to make a quick draw, but figured he would rely on his brother if ever he faced trouble. Carl remembered that there had been rumours that Arnie's pa had been Marvin Slaney who was the first owner of the saloon. Slaney had mysteriously disappeared, so perhaps Bandy had heard the rumours as well.

'Howdy, our new deputy,' said Arnie, exposing his blackened teeth. 'It's good that the law is here to protect us from any of those evil outsiders, isn't it, Ike? You know like those mean-faced dudes who we've seen in here. They look as though they would kill a man just for staring at them.'

'It sure is comforting, brother,' said Ike, 'to know that the deputy here knows all about killers, him being one himself. It takes a special sort of evil to kill a best friend, but then again he is the son of the evil bastard who shot a sweet little princess like Lucy Morgan.'

Carl knew that he had a decision to make and it wasn't easy. His instinct was to give these two son of a bitches a good beating and he would have, had he not been wearing a badge. He had to be cool, but he just couldn't let these two badmouth him every time he met them. Carl moved real close to Ike. Close enough to feel his bad breath. Ike flinched as though expecting a headbutt and he seemed unsettled when Carl smiled.

'Boys,' he said and then lowered his voice. 'I've got some advice for you. It's simple. The next time we meet, don't speak to me and don't ever let me hear you mention my Pa.'

'We're not scared of you, Brannigan. Are we, Ike?' said Arnie, who had started blinking.

'Why should we be?' his brother replied without really answering.

'Boys, don't make the mistake of thinking I won't give you a good going over on account of me wearing this badge, because I will and you aren't exactly a Johno. I expect you've heard what I did to him. And if you really believe that I killed Mark Henshall then you know what I'm capable of.'

'You can't threaten us,' mumbled Arnie, while his face reddened even more.

'I just did, Arnie. I'm leaving now unless you want to pick a fight with a law officer.'

Carl waited and then said, 'You boys

are not as dumb as you look. Enjoy your beer.'

He turned and walked away. He was still smiling when he reached the door and stepped out on to the street.

8

Joe Harper and Kyle Mason dismounted outside Margo's and tied their horses to the vacant hitch rail. Joe smiled at the girl who was about to enter the saloon and then nudged Kyle, 'I told you this was an OK place and worth coming to for easy money.'

Kyle scowled, and said, 'There're plenty of women back in Gosher County.'

'We'll have a bit of fun, do the job tomorrow and be back in Gosher soon enough.'

Joe was a lady's man and knew it. He paid a lot of attention to his black curly hair and his thin moustache and he'd already spotted the barber's shop across the street where he'd be heading for later. He was slim hipped and had wide shoulders, unlike his partner who was squat. Kyle always seemed to be brooding about something and he had no need to bother with barbers, preferring to keep his bushy beard untrimmed, and his bald head required no attention. Kyle's eyes were his most distinguishing feature, being dark, cold and owl like.

'Let's check in at the hotel, and remember, I'm Will Brooks and you're Steve Danson. We're both railroad surveyors just like we were when we did the last job. If anyone gets nosey we tell them that we're on our way to Torson Marshes. It's about fifty miles north of here and it's not on the railroad yet.'

'Why can't we just do the job now and get out of here?' Kyle moaned.

'Kyle, we've been through this before. Why risk a successful partnership? How many jobs have we done?'

'I've never thought about it, but I guess it must be about twenty,' replied Kyle thinking what did it really matter how many people he'd killed or beaten up.

'Well I reckon that it must be nearer

to thirty. We've made a lot of money and we've never come close to getting caught as far as we know. That's because we're careful. We agreed that you leave the organizing to me and the other stuff is for you to take care off with me to back you. Now let's get to the hotel and then maybe you can have a few beers while I'm at the barber's.'

The manager of the Maple Hotel checked in his latest guests and handed them the keys to rooms eight and nine. They'd walked away from the reception desk when he shouted after them.

'If you don't mind me saying so, you don't exactly look like railroad survey-ors. I guess it must be a dangerous business for one of you to be carrying two pistols.'

'Mouthy bastard,' muttered Kyle.

Joe turned and smiled at the manager and said, 'I'm the surveyor and Mister Danson looks after security. You'd be surprised how some folks resent progress and object to our work that helps expand the railroad.'

'Well, this town is better for having the railroad come to us,' the manager said and continued his glowing praise of the railroad even after Joe and Kyle were out of earshot.

★ ★ ★

Joe joined his partner in Margo's after his visit to the barber's shop and he was thinking that he'd arrived just in time. Kyle couldn't take his liquor very well, at least the amounts that he consumed. Joe had tried to work out the signs as to how it affected his partner. It never made him happy, but occasionally he seemed slightly relaxed. Now Kyle was in one of his dark moods.

'See that dude sitting near the piano?' Kyle said with a nod of his head. 'Well if he doesn't stop staring at me I'm going to take his eyes out with this glass.'

'Easy, Kyle. Maybe we need to go and get something to eat at the diner down the street. Likely the feller thinks you remind him of somebody and it's as simple as that.'

Kyle swayed when he lifted the drink to his lips and then placed it back on the bar with a bang, causing a man nearby to jump nervously.

Kyle had been pondering on what Joe had suggested and finally said, 'Well I've never seen anyone that looks anything like me, so why should the feller over there? I think he's just looking for trouble. Anyway, my belly needs filling so let's do as you say and go and get some grub, but I'm going to do that feller if he's still there when we get back'

Joe decided to forget about getting his own drink, eager to get out of the bar before Kyle ruined things and cost them a lot of money.

'You need to watch where you're going, deputy,' Kyle threatened as they nearly collided pushing through the saloon doors.

He wasn't pleased that he didn't get a response and was thinking of going back inside until Joe pushed him forward.

'Was that our man?' asked Kyle as they crossed the street.

'I don't think so,' replied Joe and added, 'but I didn't get a proper look at him.'

They were about to enter the small café when Kyle asked, 'What's this feller supposed to have done?'

'All I know is that he killed someone who was related to the man who's paying us. He wants him dead and he wants us to make sure that we don't get caught and end up being linked to him. So remember, there mustn't be any confrontation or goading like you did with that feller in Briers Peak to make him draw first. Keep it simple. We do it after dark tomorrow night. Just shoot him from behind, finish him off and we ride out of here and go and collect our money.'

Joe hadn't told Kyle that the man who had hired them had changed his mind. Joe had told the man who had passed them the message to go back and tell him that he couldn't find them. Joe had a strict rule that once he was hired then the job would be carried out. He reminded the messenger that he'd made that clear when he handed over the first instalment.

After their meal Joe and Kyle headed across the street towards the saloon and Joe was pleased when Kyle said he was going back to the hotel because the meal or the beer he'd had earlier had given him an almighty belly ache. Joe sympathized with him and said that he would see him in the morning. He watched Kyle walk slowly in the direction of the hotel and then rushed to the saloon with a spring in his step and thinking lady luck had come to his rescue. Now he could enjoy himself without worrying about the unpredictable Kyle. Joe had already decided that once this job was over and they'd been paid the second instalment he was going to ditch Kyle and find another partner. The only problem was he knew

Kyle Mason wasn't the sort to agree to a friendly break-up. If Joe did a runner he would come looking for him. So he would have no choice but to kill Kyle.

* * *

Joe wasn't too impressed by the selection of girls that he'd been studying for the last hour while he'd quietly sipped his beer. Margo had tried to get him interested in Natasha, who actually looked part Indian. He was usually partial to dusky women, but Joe decided that the woman with the huge breasts was either carrying too much weight around her middle or she would be giving birth in the coming months. He had settled on Gloria and cursed to himself when he'd seen her snuggling up to the lanky looking deputy. He was certain it was the same one that Kyle had nearly bumped into earlier and he definitely wasn't the man they'd been paid to kill.

Joe was still considering which girl

would be his second choice when Joanne sidled up to him and a quick look up and down her stunning body had him wondering why he hadn't noticed her sooner. He wished she hadn't smiled and shown that her front tooth was missing, but that didn't stop him following her upstairs.

★   ★   ★

Joe was disappointed when he made his way back to the bar after spending an hour with Joanne. He'd wanted to spend the night with her, but she'd explained that Margo had booked her to spend it with some important man from the railroad company. She seemed eager to explain that she would be free tomorrow night, but Joe told her that he would be moving on.

He had just ordered a beer when he heard a raised voice some distance away. He winced when he realized it was Kyle's and headed towards him. He was arguing with the man who he'd felt was staring at him earlier. Joe was a few tables away from Kyle when he saw him smash a glass into the man's face. Before he had dropped to the ground Joe saw the deputy draw his pistol and say something to Kyle. Kyle's gun was barely out of its holster when the deputy fired at Kyle causing him to fall beside the man with the disfigured face. The sight of the man's wounds caused Joe to cringe, but at least he was alive, unlike Kyle who lay beside him with a bullet through his heart and blood seeping through his shirt.

Joe had retreated to where he'd ordered his beer when he heard the deputy shout, 'Someone get Doc Aubrey.'

It wasn't the deputy Joe had seen talking to Gloria. It was the man they'd come to kill.

9

Carl was putting the last rifle back in the glass case when a tall man, wearing a city suit came into the office.

Marshal Dodds looked up from the wanted poster he was studying and greeted the man who had approached his desk,

'Howdy, Mister Morgan. If you've come to complain about me employing Brannigan as a deputy then you're wasting your time. I expect you've heard about his pa likely being the one that shot little Lucy.'

Dodds turned to Carl and said, 'Brannigan, this is Mister Bryn Morgan, Lucy's uncle. He's been out of town on business these past two weeks.'

'I haven't come to complain about the new deputy. I've come to tell you that whatever caused Henry Brannigan to take his life, it had nothing to do with my niece's death or the bank robbery.'

The marshal paused before he said, 'I don't know what you've been told about Henry's death, but there seems little doubt that he was involved in the robbery and with what happened to Lucy. He must have been the man on the roof who fired the shot. Even Brannigan agrees that is what must have happened.'

'Than I'm afraid he's doing his late father a disservice. Your opinions can only be based on speculation, but mine are based on fact. While the bank was being robbed Henry was in my store. We heard the shots and went outside and saw little Lucy lying on the ground. The two robbers had just mounted their horses and were riding off. The shot that killed her was fired by someone on the rooftop opposite. I ran to help Lucy and Henry ran across the street to the building from where the shot had been fired. He told me later that he saw the man running down the alley, but didn't get a proper look at him.'

Marshal Dodds looked sympathetically towards Carl and said, 'It looks like we've got a mystery on our hands, Brannigan, but it doesn't mean that your pa wasn't involved in some way, although you must be glad to hear that he didn't fire the fatal shot. It's a pity Mr Morgan has been away these past weeks because it would have stopped folks bad mouthing your pa's name and giving you a hard time.'

Bryn Morgan looked a mite angry when he asked. 'And what about the Collins brothers, Marshal? I'm still certain they were the two men that came out of the bank and rode away. Have you questioned them?'

'I questioned them as soon as I got back from my trip to kinfolk the day after the robbery when you told me you suspected it was them.'

'And what did the pair of no-goods say?' Bryn Morgan asked impatiently without waiting for the marshal to report on his questioning of the Collins brothers.

'They told me that they heard the shots while Arnie was in bed with Lily from the saloon and Ike was looking on, waiting for his turn. I didn't get a chance to ask Lily because she'd already left on the morning stagecoach. According to Milo the barman she had been planning to leave for several weeks. He said that Ike and Arnie Collins had a regular thing going with Lily and he had seen them go upstairs that day, but he couldn't remember the time.'

Bryn Morgan's face reddened some more and he muttered something about them both having a double if it wasn't them and turned away from the desk.

'I'm obliged for your support, Mr Morgan. It's much appreciated,' called Carl as Bryn Morgan reached the door.

Morgan turned and said, 'If you want to show your appreciation, Deputy, then find the man who was on the roof and make sure that he hangs or dies from a bullet.'

The silence was broken after Bryn Morgan left when WJ addressed Carl.

'Well, I'll be damned. So how come your pa had that money and why did he kill himself?'

The marshal looked at WJ and said, 'Maybe Henry Brannigan didn't kill himself. Perhaps he was murdered and his killer planted the bank money near him.'

Carl had been thinking the same thing, but why would anyone do that? Marshal Dodds was about to give the most likely reason.

'Henry might have recognized one or more of the robbers and they must have feared that he would reveal them.'

'I can understand that, Marshal,' Carl agreed. 'But it doesn't explain why Pa didn't turn Lucy's killer in before they got to him, or why his killer or killers waited so long to silence him.'

WJ decided to offer his own opinion and said, 'Mister Morgan just said your pa wasn't certain enough, or maybe the robber only thought he'd been recognized by him. Perhaps the robber just decided not to take a chance.'

WJ looked pleased with himself when the marshal said, 'WJ, you might get to be a lawman after all.' The marshal didn't spare Carl's feelings when he added, 'It's possible that it's connected with your homecoming, Brannigan.'

'I don't see how?' chipped in WJ, feeling sorry for Carl.

'The marshal has a point. It is a coincidence and Pa did say that he was going to tell me something about the robbery the night before he died.'

The marshal sighed. 'Unfortunately, knowing that Henry was innocent doesn't really help us get any closer to finding the robbers. The only thing we can do is to spread the word and then maybe folks will stop treating you like a leper. It's a shame that some of his friends didn't attend his funeral. I'm even feeling a mite guilty myself.'

Carl was looking forward to telling Mrs Logan that she had been right about Pa's innocence and be able to thank her again for her loyalty.

He was mulling over Bryn Morgan's

remarks about the Collins brothers being involved. While there had been a chance that his pa was connected with the robbery he'd had serious doubts about the brothers being involved, because his pa would never have teamed up with them. Things were different now, and he put a question to the marshal:

'Marshal, do you think there's a chance that the Collins boys made up that alibi about being with the saloon girl? It seems a bit odd her leaving town like she did.'

'If it was anyone else but the brothers I would have said yes. But we all know that the boys are not the brightest stars in the sky. I suppose Bryn Morgan is going to keep on about them, so although my gut feeling is that it will be a waste of time I think I'll ride over to Orton and hope that Lily is still there. That's if you two can look after things while I'm away.'

'Sure we can. Can't we, Deputy Brannigan!' said WJ, who obviously regarded himself as the senior deputy even though he knew that Carl was the more capable.

'It'll be good experience for us, Marshal,' said Carl and added, 'and at least you'll show the town council that you'll be investigating every angle.'

The marshal tapped the desk with both hands and said, 'That's settled then. I'll leave in the morning and I should be back in a couple of days. Oh, and while I'm away I don't want you two to start poking around with the robbery investigation. You'll have enough to keep you occupied. So is that clear?' The marshal had been looking at Carl while he was laying down his instructions.

'Sure thing, Marshal,' replied WJ.

'And that includes the Collins boys. Especially the Collins boys, because if I'm wrong and I find out that Lily did cover for them, then I don't want to come back and find that you've frightened them off. You understand what I'm saying, don't you, Brannigan?'

'Don't worry, Marshal, I'll give them a wide berth unless they start shooting up the town, but I can't see them doing that because we've come to an understanding.'

Carl was expecting the marshal to ask what he meant by his remarks, but he didn't. He just gathered a few things together before he wished them luck and left.

'You think the Collins boys did it, don't you, Carl?' WJ asked after the marshal had closed the door behind him.

'I'm not really sure, WJ. They're a slimy pair. Well Ike certainly is. And they never seem short of money even though they don't work, so they must be up to no good. But I wonder if even they would be dumb enough to rob the bank in their own town. I just don't know, but I'm glad the marshal is going to try and find that saloon girl.'

'Can I ask you a sort of personal question?'

Carl laughed and replied, 'As long as

it isn't about women, WJ. I'm not exactly an expert on them.'

'It's not about women. It's about your time as a deputy in, what was that place called?'

'Bugle Falls. So what's the question?'

'Did you ever kill anyone? I mean in the line of duty. I know Marshal Dodds has killed more than a few and I wondered if you have.'

'Just the one and it was in a saloon,' Carl replied and his face took on a serious look as he remembered the incident.

'What was it like?' asked WJ and then quickly said that Carl didn't have to discuss it if he didn't want to.

'No I don't mind. I take it you haven't, WJ.'

WJ shuddered and shook his head.

'It was upsetting at the time, mainly on account that the young feller wasn't what you might call a bad guy.'

'Did you have to kill him or could you have wounded him? I suppose you shot him?'

'Yes, I shot him through the back of the head. He was as close to me as you are now. I have asked myself many times whether I should have just whacked him with the butt end of my pistol. What I did seemed the right thing to do at the time, but I guess I'll have to live with it for the rest of my life.'

'So why did you have to do it. It seems odd you being so close to him and being behind him?'

'It was in a saloon. Leo Gains, the feller I shot, and his buddies had been drinking all day. They came from wealthy folks and were always flashing their money about and getting up to wild things. I was called over to the saloon because things were getting out of hand. They were having bets on who could knock back the most glasses of whiskey during the time it took for a saloon girl to sing a song. Leo accused one of his buddies of cheating and lost out in the fight that followed. He just couldn't handle the liquor and I guess he felt humiliated when his buddy got the better of him in the fight. What I mean about Leo Gains not being bad is that he wasn't like a Collins or some low life like the one I had to shoot in Margo's saloon.'

'Did you see the trouble building up?'

'No, as I said, I was sent for and when I got to the saloon Leo had just smashed a bottle over the other feller's head. He said he was going to cut the man's throat with the broken bottle he was holding. I called out to him to drop it and he just turned and said he was going to do him. I was within touching distance when he raised his arm preparing to carry out his threat and that's when I fired.'

'Jesus! It must have been a tricky decision to make. Did you save the other feller?'

Carl sighed and replied, 'I did, but someone shot him in the back two days later. We never found his killer.'

WJ looked worried. 'I know that I

might have to kill a man one day, but if I do, then I hope it's not close up. To be honest I'm not sure I could do it and I wouldn't want to let you or the marshal down by hesitating or not even firing.'

'Let me ask you a question, WJ. Why did you become a lawman?'

WJ sighed and said, 'I guess I always wanted to and I've always liked guns, but I think it was when my pa was killed. You might not remember it, but it was when he ran the livery and two fellers tried to steal horses from the corral at the back. They could have just ridden off. Pa wasn't even armed, but they shot him for fun, according to a witness. I was only ten at the time, but I can still remember watching those two men hang. I didn't want to, but my Uncle Jed made me.'

'But what's the main reason you're a lawman, WJ?' Carl asked, determined to get his buddy to be more specific.

'Well I guess it's because we need lawmen to stop people like those who killed Pa from killing others. And I feel it's important, really important that we have law and order and I get some satisfaction helping to keep the town a safer place.'

'You do it for the right reasons, WJ, and I'm sure come the day that you have to, then you'll kill a man but it will only be because it has to be done, and that's the way it should be.'

Carl meant what he'd said to WJ, but times were changing and things were happening, like his father's murder that made him wonder if he would always only kill when he had to. There would be situations where a judgement had to be reached about making a move on a son of a bitch who was considering gunning you down. Marshal Took had warned him of the dangers of trying to wound a man and risk him getting a shot off that might end your life. Carl knew that his principles and courage would be tested more and more, and he hoped that he would make the right decision when the time came.

10

Shelley Morgan had just finished placing flowers on her sister's grave when she sensed someone approaching. It was Carl Brannigan. She had hoped that she would get the chance to speak to him ever since Vincent Henshall had embarrassed her with his accusations against him on the day of Henry Brannigan's funeral. She was upset that Vincent was still insisting that Henry Brannigan was Lucy's killer despite Uncle Bryn's statement that he couldn't possibly be.

'Howdy, Miss Shelley,' Carl said, as he drew level with her on the way to visit his own folks' graves. He offered her his hand. 'I guess you remember who I am after your boyfriend's introduction.'

She blushed, lowered her eyes and replied, 'Vincent's not my boyfriend.

He's just a friend.' She blushed even more when she added, 'I don't have a boyfriend.'

'Now that does surprise me. Perhaps they don't start courtin' young from where you hail from. Where do you come from if you don't mind me asking?'

'My Daddy and Uncle Bryn come from Wales. It's a small country next to England, but my mom comes from a little town called Senintao in Nevada and that's where I was born and raised along with my little sister Lucy. Uncle Bryn has never married. He says he has too much work to do before he hands over the business to Daddy and becomes a preacher.'

'If it wasn't for your uncle speaking up the folks around here would still be thinking bad things about my pa and that wouldn't have been fair because he was a good man and not a bit like me, his only son.'

'I'm sorry for what Vincent said about you and your pa. From what folks say you're a good man as well, even if you were a bit wild when you were young.'

Carl laughed and said, 'I hope I'm still young. You mustn't believe everything that folks say.'

'I didn't mean you were old,' she said and Carl replied that he was only teasing her. 'Shelley, I'd like to take you riding and show you some real pretty country. I'd make sure that I called on your folks and asked their permission. Maybe I could call on you tomorrow morning. The marshal's away, but things should be quiet in town and my buddy, WJ, will be around to keep the peace.'

She gave him the sweetest of smiles and said, 'I'd like that and my daddy would appreciate you calling on him and Mom.'

Carl told her he would be looking forward to tomorrow and then explained that he was going to have a quick visit to his folks' graves and then head back into town and take over from his buddy.

Shelley was still at her sister's grave

when he passed by later and he raised a hand to his Stetson and said with a smile, 'I'll be seeing you real soon, Shelley.' As he walked on he saw movement in the trees some distance away. It might have been the wind that caused it, but he didn't think that it was.

* * *

Carl felt like a schoolboy as he waited for Shelley to come into the room at the back of Morgan's Store. He'd spent the last five minutes making polite conversation with her folks. They seemed nice people, but he could tell that they were nervous about their daughter going on a ride with him. Carl's first impression was that they made an odd couple. Kathryn Morgan was a tall refined looking lady. Her greying hair was immaculately groomed and held back by a pale blue ribbon and she had the same large smiling eyes that Shelley must have inherited. Her clothes were certainly not homemade like his ma's had been and she would have looked more at home amongst wealthy city folk than in this mid-town store. William Morgan was a good four inches shorter than his wife. He had a ruddy face that still showed the strain of his recent sorrow and a rotund figure of a man with an appetite for more home cooking than was good for him.

'Your work must be dangerous at times,' suggested Kathryn Morgan.

'Only if you get careless, ma'am. Most of the cowboys are too drunk when they start being a nuisance so there's not much chance of them causing you any harm.'

William Morgan asked Carl if he was a drinking man and received a disapproving glare from his wife.

'I do like a beer and a good night out from time to time, sir, but Marshal Dodds wouldn't tolerate anyone drinking while they were on duty, except on very special occasions. I take it you don't approve of liquor, Mister Morgan?'

'Only in moderation. Our father saw drink cause a lot of misery back in the village we lived in and never allowed me and my brother to drink while we were living under his roof.'

'Here she is,' Kathryn announced and gave Shelley an approving look as she came into the room wearing her riding clothes. Carl stood up, relieved that the questions would stop. It felt like he was being assessed in some way as to his suitability to keep their daughter company. He didn't know if this was just the Morgans' way of trying to protect their daughter, or if this was normal because despite his age it was his first experience of such a thing.

By the time they had ridden a short distance out of town heading for the trail that would take them to the Grove Hills, Carl could see that Shelley was a fine horsewoman. She explained later that she had been taught by her mother whose family had bred horses on their Nevada Ranch. He'd suggested taking her to the Grove Hills above the Hen-shall and Brannigan ranches because it was the highest point for miles and she hadn't been this far before. They'd ridden mostly in silence, with the occasional sidelong glance, but when they stopped near the lonely yew tree at the top of the hill she told him she hadn't realized that there was such beauty so close to Maple.

As he helped her down from her white mare he said, 'I'm surprised that Vincent hasn't brought you up here.'

'He wanted to do just a few weeks ago, but I told him that Daddy wouldn't allow me to come this far out of the town. Vincent would like us to become more than friends and I don't want that. He's been kind to me since my sister was killed, but I will never see him as more than just a friend and he is a lot older than me. I know my mom likes the idea of me seeing Vincent, and I'm afraid I lied to him about daddy not approving of me riding out this far.'

'Miss Morgan, shame on you,' he teased and then led the horses closer to the tree and tied their reins to it. He suggested they took a stroll so that he could point out the boundaries of the two ranches below.

'Were you really good friends with Vincent's brother and is it true you argued over a girl?'

Carl screwed his face and tucked in his chin to create a look of surprise. 'You do ask direct questions, but so do your folks. I suppose you get it off them.' He smiled making it clear that he wasn't offended by the question and replied, 'The answer to both questions is yes, but did Vincent tell you that he was also interested in Isobel Clayman, the girl that Mark and me argued over?'

'No, Vincent never mentioned her by name or that he even liked her.'

'Poor Vincent!' said Carl and shook his head as he cast his mind back. 'He was really serious about her, but to me and Mark she was just a bit of fun and it would have stayed that way had we not been stupid and drunk more liquor than was good for us that night.'

'Was she beautiful?' Shelley asked.

'She was, if you liked women with a scrawny neck, straggly hair and their front teeth missing. You know the sort of woman that Vincent is attracted to.'

Shelley gave him a playful tap with her riding gloves before he said, 'I suppose she was, but we were all very young and Maple didn't have too many women of our age, apart from the saloon girls. Anyway, let me explain a few landmarks to you.'

He pointed out the River Tundry snaking its way into the distance and the tributary that led off on to the Henshall land. The sky was clear and they had a good view of the Henshall's magnificent ranch-house in the distance and she was impressed by that.

'So who owns the river?' Shelley asked.

Carl smiled and answered, 'No one owns the river. Most of the stretch we see below divides Pa's ranch from the Henshall's property.' It still didn't feel right calling it his ranch, and he guessed it never would.

'Vincent said something about your pa not being willing to pay to use the water on his land. Why couldn't your cattle get their water from the main river if nobody owns it?'

'Because it's too fast flowing for the cattle to drink from even in the shallow section and they would be in danger of being drowned if they were swept away into deeper water. It wasn't just the water that we needed. The Henshall land is twenty times bigger than what Pa owned and when he built up his herd Theodore Henshall gave permission for Pa to graze his cows on Henshall land for free.'

Carl didn't want to risk boring this lovely girl with talk of ranching matters and said, 'Anyway, let's make our way back to the horses. I expect your Daddy will be staring at a clock by now.'

She'd smiled when he'd added that he didn't want to get into her pa's bad books because he hoped she'd come out with him again. He took her silence to mean that she would like that. She asked if he could point out his ranch house and he told her there wasn't one anymore and he would explain why some other time.

When they reached the yew tree he held her hand and felt like a young boy once again when he asked if he could kiss her. She blushed and replied that she had never been asked such a question before. He smiled and told her that he'd never asked it either. He kissed her just for a moment and he felt her body stiffen with pleasure as she gave a gentle moan. They hugged each other until he finally released her and helped her climb on to her horse. They rode home, each of them knowing that they had met someone special.

11

The first night of Marshal Dodds's absence was uneventful, but both the deputies knew that the real test would be tonight. Saturday night was the time when the town filled up with drifters and even if there were no cattle drives close by the saloons would be full, and there would always be some fighting over a saloon girl. Margo had wanted to employ her own 'heavies' to keep things in order, but Marshal Dodds had ruled that there was only one law enforcement in town and that was under his control.

★ ★ ★

WJ and Carl had become increasingly uneasy as they had watched the men riding into town and it was only mid-afternoon when Carl brought the first troublemakers back to the cells. WJ looked worried when Carl approached the marshal's desk after locking up the men. One of them had pulled his gun on the barman in Margo's, claiming that he'd served him watery beer. The other feller was already as drunk as a skunk and he'd threatened to shoot the place up if they didn't get their money back.

'Carl, maybe it would have been better if the marshal had gone looking for Lily at the beginning of the week and then he'd be here now. I've got a bad feeling about tonight, buddy. I saw one group ride in this afternoon and I just know they're going to give us some grief.'

Carl shook his head and smiled, 'You worry too much, WJ. If they step out of line we'll just lock them up.'

'Aren't you forgetting that we already have two in the cells and things haven't even started to warm up yet!'

Carl had a solution to the problem of overcrowded cells and explained it to WJ. 'So if the cells become full we'll release the less serious troublemakers, but hold on to their weapons and money. We tell them to go sleep it off somewhere and come back for their belongings in the morning. And we make it clear to them that if they step out of line again then we'll escort them to the edge of town, make them strip naked and leave them there. It'll get mighty cold tonight so at least they won't be bothering any saloon girls when their manhood turns blue.'

WJ laughed, but soon became serious when he said that the marshal wouldn't approve of Carl's methods.

'The marshal isn't here, WJ, and he'll want us to use our initiative. You know, work things out on our own. This is our little test and to be honest I'm looking forward to it. Talking of the marshal, I saw the Collins boys ride in earlier and they had fine looking new horses and fancy saddles. I've never seen Ike wearing anything but black until today, but he had a new denim suit to match his brother's.'

WJ looked thoughtful again and said, 'I wonder where they got the money from because as far as I know they don't do any work. They just slob around that cabin of theirs near the old mine and they've got no kinfolk to provide for them.'

Carl sighed and shook his head and sounded like the marshal when he said, 'Don't be a dope, WJ. If Bryn Morgan's right, then they've been spending some of the bank robbery money.'

'But that would attract attention to them, wouldn't it?' said WJ.

Carl ignored his buddy's comment. 'I've got an idea, WJ, but I really need your help.'

When Carl had finished explaining it to him, WJ shook his head and said, 'No chance! The marshal would kick your butt if you went riding out and searched the Collins place. And you'd be leaving me here on my own when we both know there's trouble brewing.'

Carl felt disappointed and he said, 'You're right, buddy. It wouldn't be fair on you, but I may not get a better opportunity than this to find out who killed my pa and that little girl. There's a good chance that the marshal will come home tomorrow and tell us that Lily the saloon girl has moved on. That's what most of these girls do when they get fed up of being mauled by the same smelly cowboys. I guess they're hoping that they'll meet some rich sucker who'll offer them a new life.'

'Hmm,' WJ sighed as he considered Carl's proposal some more and then said, 'I suppose the Collins boys will stay in town until the saloons close and if you left now you'd be back before the real action started, but I'm still not sure about this.'

Carl tried a final bit of persuasion when he said, 'If things go wrong I'll make sure that the marshal knows that this was my idea and you knew nothing about it, WJ. I promise you that you won't lose your job over this. If I don't find anything then we needn't tell the marshal, and if I do then he'll have a moan, but he'll be pleased.'

'That's right,' said WJ and added, 'we'll say we used our, what was that word you used?'

Carl smiled and said, 'Initiative,'

'That's it, initiative. Did you learn that big word on your travels?'

Carl smiled. 'I learned it at the same place you would have done had you not been too busy gawping at Beth Ross during Mrs Hogan's lessons.'

'I wonder what happened to Beth?' said WJ and added, 'I expect she married some rich dude. She sure was a good looking woman. She reminds me a bit of Shelley Morgan. That Vincent Henshall is a lucky guy.'

Carl hadn't told him that he'd been seeing Shelley and he decided not to mention that Vincent had no chance with her.

'I'd better get out to the Collins place, WJ. Now don't you go being a hero while I'm away.'

'I won't. Good luck, buddy,' replied

WJ trying to hide the worry that was building up inside him.

* * *

Carl had only been to the Collins cabin once and that had been over ten years ago when he'd gone with his pa to buy a horse off Bandy Collins. It had been a lovely animal and Pa planned to use it for breeding, and then he discovered it had been stolen and Bandy Collins wasn't the rightful owner. Collins had said that he'd bought it in good faith and offered to pay Henry back, but he never did. Carl remembered giving Ike Collins a bloody nose after the brothers had picked on a little kid after school. Not that the boys attended school very often. There'd been a rumour a few years before he'd left that the brothers had beaten a cowboy to death down an alleyway near the saloon. Ike had been seen with the cowboy's stolen money bag and Bandy Collins had sworn that his sons had stayed at home that night.

Ike had claimed that he'd found the empty wallet when he'd ridden into town some days later. Everyone knew that the boys were no-good thieves, but they could never prove a case against them. Carl was hoping that the Collins's luck and scheming ways was about to end.

He hadn't taken much notice of the place all those years ago, but it must have been better than it was now. Bandy had died shortly before Carl had left town and you didn't have to be a doctor to know that he'd drunk himself to death because his skin was as yellow as a China man's.

Carl couldn't remember them having a dog, but they did now and it was growling more than barking as it pulled on the chain that secured it to the large wooden kennel. He had never seen a meaner looking dog that was as wide as it was tall. He figured it was a mixed breed, but mostly terrier with a massive head and sturdy legs. The scrawny chicken that hurried away had been

110

neglected, but the black and tan coloured dog hadn't. As he dismounted outside the cabin he caught some movement from the corner of his eye. If he was a betting man he would have wagered it was a large rat. The badly fitted front door was in danger of falling apart as he pushed it open and the dog's low growling turned into a frantic barking. Carl drew his pistol as a precaution in case the chain holding it snapped, or it pulled away the rotten wood of the kennel it was secured to.

The brothers always seemed reasonably well dressed, but the inside of the cabin had the smell of a cell on a Sunday morning which was a mixture made up of puke, body odour, stale food and urine. Carl scanned the floor hoping to find evidence of a loose floor board, but none was obvious. He picked up an old rifle that was on the table and probably in the process of being cleaned and used it to lift the thin, badly stained mattress off the only bed in the cabin. He found a number of dollar bills, but he didn't need to count them to realise that it wasn't what he was looking for. He used the rifle to remove any item that might be covering a hiding place before he gave up and went outside into the fresh air. He stepped back when the animal's ferocity increased even further. Carl was thinking that the Collins boys wouldn't be the sort to have visitors, or be worried if the dog mauled any one that came here uninvited, so why chain the animal up! Why not just let it roam free and guard the cabin, or just leave it inside? The only thing the dog was protecting was the kennel, or anything that might be hidden inside it. Would the brothers be that clever, he thought, and decided that Ike might. Carl had come across hill-billy folk who couldn't read or write and had a strange doziness about them, but they were wise about certain things and a match for any city slicker when it came to raw cunning. Carl needed to check inside the kennel. He thought about catching and killing the chicken and tossing it to the dog to distract it, but decided the chicken would have been finished off before he had got very far with his search. There was also the chance that the dog would prefer a chunk of his leg rather than the chicken. Carl pulled out his pistol. He'd decided that he wouldn't leave here without searching the kennel. He would have to kill the dog!

12

WJ looked at the wall clock in the marshal's office for the fifth time in as many minutes. It had been over two hours since Carl had ridden off. Something had definitely gone wrong. The question was what! He had a decision to make. Should he ride out to the Collins place or start doing his rounds. The decision was made for him when Fingers Malone, the pianist from Margo's, burst in. 'Where's the marshal? Margo said for him to get off his fat butt and come over to the saloon. There's real trouble about to break out because some cowboys have been knocking back liquor they've brought into the saloon.'

'The marshal's away on business, but tell her I'll be over soon,' said WJ.

Malone shook his head. 'I ain't telling her that because she'll only send me over here again. I best tell that you're on your way.'

'OK, I'll be right behind you,' said WJ. His worst fears had just come true.

Malone hurried out of the door and WJ looked at the clock and groaned: 'Where are you Carl, buddy?' Then he scolded himself, checked his gun, grabbed his hat and headed for Margo's saloon.

He'd never seen the place this full, or Margo looking so angry as she headed towards him. 'Why haven't you lazy good for nothings been over here?'

'The marshal and my buddy Carl are away on important business, but I'm here now. So what's your problem, Margo? I'll try and sort it out, but I would rather wait for Carl to get back, if that's OK.'

'No, it's not OK. That lot over by the piano are swigging back liquor they didn't buy in here, which is against the house rules. I've asked them nicely to stop and they told me to go and stick my head in a piss pot. Now they're selling the liquor to other customers. My barman might as well take the night off. Well this isn't a charity hall and I don't pay the town council good money for nothing in return. You sort them out now, or I'll take a pistol to them myself.'

'All right, Margo. I'll go and speak to them,' said WJ trying to calm her and himself down, because his heart was thumping.

'He's going to speak to them,' groaned Margo before she looked towards the ceiling and hurried away.

'Hey, Deputy! Pull up a chair and have a drink with us,' said the big feller dressed in a fancy silk shirt when he saw WJ approach him. His cheesy smile revealed a couple of gold teeth to match the three large rings on each hand. WJ was feeling uneasy when the man mentioned that he'd heard that the marshal had gone away and mightn't be coming back. WJ looked at the giant clock on the wall behind the piano and quietly cursed Carl for leaving him in the lurch when he knew that trouble was likely. He considered drawing his pistol and remembered the marshal saying about never pointing a gun at someone unless you aim to use it, so he relaxed his hand and opted to try and talk his way through a solution.

'Margo tells me that she's asked you to stop selling liquor and she's explained that it's against the house rules. If you stop now and put your own booze away then I won't take it any further.'

The man smiled and said, 'Well that's generous of you, Deputy, but unless you've got a small army of lawmen outside I suggest you hurry back over the street and lock your door because we aim to carry on selling. We're giving folk what they want and there's no harm in that. If that old bitch Margo can't compete with our prices then that's her problem. Anyway, what's she got to complain about? Most of these suckers will soon be ready to take one of her girls upstairs, even though some of them will be in no state to find their manhood, let alone use it. One of them might even fancy giving Margo a good seeing to, but I think this liquor would have to be a lot stronger before anyone would fancy that painted witch.'

'So you're not going to stop then?' WJ asked, knowing that his voice sounded nervous and lacked any authority.

'We don't aim to stay here all night,' he replied and WJ was hopeful for a moment until he heard the words, 'Just until someone throws us out, or we have no liquor left.'

Everyone laughed, but when they stopped one of the men said, 'I think this greenhorn deputy is hitching to pull his gun on you, Scully. He aims for you to do your sleeping off in the cells and not upstairs in a warm bed with one of the girls.'

Scully stood up, blew cigar smoke into WJ's face and then pulled his head away and then delivered a vicious headbutt to the bridge of WJ's nose. The blow caused WJ to stumble and smash his face against the table top.

'A couple of you boys better see that the deputy gets back to his office,' Scully said with a snigger and sat down.

Those around the table laughed again and two of them stood up. One of them asked, 'Do you want him roughed up some more, Scully?'

'If you want to, but not too much. He isn't going to cause us any bother,' replied the ringleader and then wiped some of WJ's blood from his shirt.

The two men dragged the unconscious WJ across the saloon floor and out on to the sidewalk outside the saloon. WJ started vomiting and one of the men took pity on him and said, 'Let's leave him here. I think he's had enough and he needs some help.'

* * *

Carl was feeling pleased with himself on the way back to town. What did they say in the military, mission accomplished? Marshal Dodds might be a bit riled if he'd found Lily and she'd confessed to covering for the Collins brothers, but some slippery legal dude might object to the evidence of a saloon girl. At least there was no way that they could wriggle out of the charges now that he'd recovered the money and he had the evidence to link the brothers to the robbery. It had taken him longer than he'd expected, but he would still be back in town within the hour, or so he thought.

* * *

Carl was only a mile from the Collins place and deep in thought, thinking about Shelley Morgan and what his discovery might mean to her family, when he heard the gunshot and his horse crumpled to the ground. He hit the soft trail with a thud and for a moment he was winded and unable to think properly. He shook his head and it helped clear his drowsiness and he crouched behind the fallen animal in the hope it might provide some protection, but he knew that he was a sitting duck. He pulled his rifle from the scabbard and scanned the area. The light was fading and he could see a number of places where the shot could have been fired from and he expected a second one to follow, but it didn't.

The wounded horse would soon be dead, because the bullet must have hit a main vein judging by the amount of blood that was being gently pumped into the sand. He saw no point in prolonging its suffering and fired a bullet into its head. It had been a good horse and it held many memories of his time at home and particularly of his pa. He squinted at his watch in the dim light. There was no way he would make it back to town before the trouble started unless a rider came his way. He would move as quickly as possible and hope that whoever took the shot at him thought he was dead and had ridden off.

★　★　★

The trail into town had been reasonably flat and mostly smooth, but by the time Carl reached the start of Main Street his feet were throbbing and he was exhausted. He needed to go and find WJ as quickly as possible, but first of all he would find a safe place for the stolen money that was in his saddle-bag.

* * *

Bryn Morgan looked up from the ledger he'd been writing in and gestured to whoever was hammering on his door to go away.

'We're closed,' he shouted and then when the hammering continued threw his pen down in anger, picked up the pistol from under the counter and headed for the door. Perhaps the gun would encourage the drunken cowboy to move on. It wasn't the first time this had happened and perhaps he shouldn't have done the stocktaking on a Saturday night. He made a mental note that he wouldn't do that in future.

He drew back the bolts after he'd recognized Carl, but he still wasn't happy.

'Just because you're the law doesn't mean you can disturb folks at this time of night.'

Carl decided it might help if he pulled out the bank bag, and it did; prompting Bryn to say, 'You'd better come in.'

Carl quickly explained that Bryn Morgan had been right about the Collins boys and that he was in a hurry and needed a safe place for the money. Morgan offered to put it in the store's safe, but insisted that they count it first. Soon Carl was hurrying towards the marshal's office and the five-thousand dollars were locked away in the safe. He'd spotted a few cowboys who were trying to brawl, but were too drunk to harm each other. Things looked quiet and then he saw the crowd outside Margo's where Doc Aubrey was attending to a man lying on the ground. He decided to forget about dropping his saddle-bag at the marshal's office and checking to see if WJ was there. As he drew close to the crowd they separated and he was able to see the bloodied face of WJ.

'What's happened to him?' Carl asked, anxiously.

'Don't worry, Carl,' said Doc Aubrey. 'He's just come round and that's the main thing. He'll be right as rain in a couple of days and he'll soon have his good looks back.'

'Will he be all right on his own, doc?' Carl asked, feeling guilty as hell.

The doc confirmed that he would, and Carl asked for two men to carry WJ over to the marshal's office and lay him on a bed in one of the opened cells. Carl figured that at least he would be able to keep looking in on him in between doing his rounds. After the two volunteers had carried WJ away, accompanied by Doc Aubrey, Carl addressed the gathering and asked if anyone knew who had beaten up WJ, but he was greeted with silence.

'One of you must have seen it, you cowardly bunch,' he snapped angrily as he looked into the eyes of each man.

One man lowered his voice and looked frightened as he said, 'It was a feller named Scully and he's still inside Margo's with his gang. They've been causing trouble all night. He's the guy with gold rings on most of his fingers. He's sat over by the piano or at least he was earlier.'

Carl relaxed a little and said: 'You'll sleep better tonight, my friend, for having the guts to tell me what happened,' and then headed for the saloon door and pushed it open with a force that was driven by his anger against the man on whom he intended to inflict serious harm.

Carl ignored the advancing Margo and headed for the table near the piano. By the time Scully saw him emerge from behind the group in front of his table Carl had already drawn his gun. He grabbed the back of Scully's head and rammed his face against the hard table while roaring out to the others, 'If you move I'll blow your bastard heads off.' The men froze as they watched Scully's face hit the table top over and over again and saw his blood mix with the spilt liquor. Scully was groaning when Carl placed the troublemaker's hand on the table and then used Scully's own pistol like a hammer to smash the fingers of his gun hand.

Carl ordered the men to drop their gunbelts and then said, 'Now you take this son of a bitch and leave town. If any of you set foot in Maple again then I'll shoot you on sight and that's a promise. Now move.'

Margo was smiling when she approached, ready to thank him, but he walked away saying, 'Not now, Margo. I want to see these no-goods leave town and then I need to check on my buddy.'

★   ★   ★

Doc Aubrey came out of the office as Carl stepped on to the sidewalk and told him that he'd given WJ a half a mug of whiskey to drink and he'd soon be asleep. So Carl wasn't alarmed when he looked in on him a few minutes later and was greeted by loud snoring. But Carl was surprised and annoyed when he saw that WJ must have arrested another two men after he'd gone to the Collins's place and the men were asleep. Carl had plans for that cell and he unlocked it and then shook both the cowboys awake, or at least half awake and then asked them why WJ had arrested them, hoping it wasn't anything too serious.

'We were only cuddling a couple of the girls. We didn't mean any harm,' one of them replied.

Carl knew that they must have been doing a lot more than cuddling. He told them they could go, but ordered them to stay out of the saloons tonight. He had a feeling that they would have been happy to have remained asleep in the cells as they trudged towards the door after he had given them back their pistols.

Carl followed them out and shouted after them, 'If I see you in a saloon later then I'll give you a good kicking.'

'Right, now for the serious business,' said Carl to himself as he closed the office door and headed back to Margo's.

The bar was still lively, but a mite quieter than during his previous visit. The faces looking in his direction included admiring looks from the saloon girls, men giving him a friendly nod and others showing that they were wary of him. They would have seen his determined expression as he made directly to the far end of the bar where the Collins brothers were standing. The table nearby was still showing some of Scully's blood and Ike and Arnie who had witnessed Carl inflict so much pain on Scully now looked nervous as he stood in front of them.

'We're just having a quiet beer, Deputy, and we're not looking for trouble,' said Arnie

'That's a fine looking dog you boys have,' said Carl in a casual manner, 'I don't suppose you have much to worry about with him guarding your property while you're in town having a quiet drink and enjoying yourselves.'

'He's a bull terrier. His name's Killerboy,' said Arnie with a snigger. 'He used to fight other dogs in a ring. We saw him kill three dogs over at Shamuna. It wasn't fair matching him three to one, but he ended up the winner. When we were leaving the show we found him and he was in a mess so we brought him home. The bastard who abandoned the dog must have figured he'd be no good for fighting anymore, but Ike got him better.'

'When did you see our dog?' Ike asked showing more concern than his babbling brother.

'Just a couple of hours ago. I called in to have a little talk with you boys, but you must have been in town. But it wasn't a wasted journey.'

Ike was getting agitated now and asked, 'Did you kill our dog, Brannigan?' and without waiting for a reply shouted out,

'You did, didn't you?'

'Why would I want to kill your dog? He couldn't reach me to stop me looking around your little palace.'

'It ain't right to go prying around people's private property,' said Ike, his face wild with anger.

'You could say I was prying, but I suppose it was more of a search. Anyway, I didn't find what I was looking for.' Carl paused and then added, 'At least not in the cabin, but there were lots of other little hiding places like those sheds at the back, including the one you boys use for shitting in. Although judging by the state of the cabin you might just as well do it in there.'

'What do you want with us, Deputy?' asked Ike as he wiped the sweat from his brow.

'I'll tell you in a minute because I'm getting a bit bored with this chin-wag. I'm here because Marshal Dodds has just come back. He's waiting outside for you boys and he asked me to come and get you.'

'Why?' Arnie asked.

'Well, it's probably got something to do with that bag of money I found hidden under the floor of your friendly dog's kennel.'

'You did kill him, you bastard,' Ike cursed. 'There's no way the dog would've let you near the kennel, so you must've killed him. We'll get you for this, Brannigan. One way or the other we'll get you. Maybe we might arrange for you to lose someone you're fond of, like that Shelley Morgan. Anyway, we ain't moving, and if the marshal wants us, then let him come and get us, messenger boy.'

Carl moved closer to them as though he was ready to confide something to them. He lowered his voice, 'Ike, I want you and your brother to walk out of here nice and quietly, and no one will get hurt. If you don't, I'm going to pull my gun on you, and then I'm going to give your right hand the same treatment that I gave that Scully feller, except I'll break your fingers one at a time.'

'You're forgetting that there are two of us,' Ike said with a sneer.

Carl smiled and said, 'I think I could drink me a beer by the time your fat brother fumbled and tried to find the handle of his gun. Now start moving.'

Carl moved back a step showing his intention to draw his pistol and he kept eye contact with Ike who was pondering whether to make a move of his own until he growled, 'Let's go, Arnie. Let's go and have a talk with Marshal Dodds. He'll put this greenhorn in his place.'

Carl followed them out into the street and then pulled out his pistol and cocked it before ordering them to drop their gunbelts to the ground. There was some muttering and Ike said his weapons cost him a lot of money, but they followed the order, and dropped their belts on to the sidewalk.

Carl called out to the young cowboy who was about to enter the saloon. 'Hey, feller, take those gunbelts inside and tell Margo I'll pick them up later.'

'Where's the marshal?' asked Ike as

he looked around the street.

'He must have gone back to his office,' Carl lied and told them to move.

The brothers did a lot more threatening and grumbling when Carl locked them in the cell and they kept repeating their demands to see the marshal. Carl had been called a lot of things in his time and he reckoned the brothers had called him every one of them and a few more as well.

Carl wondered what WJ would think in the morning when he realized who was in the next cell to him. Carl was fairly certain that WJ hadn't recognized him when he saw him outside Margo's while the doctor was treating him and probably thought things had gone wrong out at the Collins place.

13

'He's not going to be pleased, Carl. I just have an uneasy feeling about this,' said WJ through his swollen lips.

Carl turned away from looking out of the office window. 'Why don't you go home and let me handle the marshal? He mightn't even return today. Perhaps he's shacked up with the saloon girl and we'll never see him again.'

'Do you think so,' WJ said hopefully. 'Then you could become the new marshal.'

'You're the senior man, WJ. I'd be your deputy.'

'I'm no fool, Carl. I know I haven't got it in me to be a marshal, but I'm no coward either and I'll stay and face the music with you. Now keep looking out for him so I can look busy when he comes in. It might put him in a good mood if he sees I've done all his paperwork.'

The deputies had drunk two mugs of coffee and played cards until they were bored before Carl announced that the marshal was riding down Main Street.

'Good, he hasn't stopped to talk to anyone,' said Carl before he hurried away from the window. WJ had vacated the marshal's seat by the time he came through the office door.

'What the hell happened to you, boy?' growled the marshal, ignoring their greetings.

'Just the usual Saturday night trouble,' replied WJ.

The marshal looked at Carl and said, 'How come your pretty face is unmarked. Didn't you back your partner up? I hope you didn't forget one of my golden rules about always operating in twos on a Saturday night.'

'Carl made sure that the feller who did this to me ended up looking much worse than I do. One group were searching under the tables to see how many teeth he'd lost. The feller who won the bet had guessed six and he was

135

the closest because they found seven.'

The marshal didn't seem impressed by WJ's attempts to make excuses for Carl.

'Did you find Lily?' asked WJ, eager to change the subject about last night after his swollen nose had begun to throb again.

'I did, and she was very cooperative,' replied the marshal with a smile.

Carl decided he might as well get it over with and said, 'Marshal, there's been a development here. The Collins boys are in the cells and they definitely did the bank robbery.'

Marshal Dodds's face turned angry as he said, 'I don't suppose they walked in here and confessed. So that means that my clear orders must have been ignored and that's one thing I can't abide. During the war I saw good and brave men killed, because some idiot couldn't follow a simple order.'

'It was all down to me, Marshal. WJ was against the idea, but I went out and searched the Collins cabin. I found a stash of money in a bag just like the one that had been planted in my pa's barn. The boys had been throwing their money about in the saloon and bought a couple of fine horses and fancy saddles.'

'So while you went searching their cabin you left your buddy on his own. Was this when he got his face messed up?

Carl hadn't expected the marshal to react this way and tried to explain some more. 'I hadn't planned to be gone for more than hour and things were quiet, but I know it was wrong.'

'You're damned right it was wrong. WJ might have got killed just because you acted on a hunch instead of waiting for me to come home today. Lily told me that the boys had threatened to carve up her face unless she lied for them. We could have been riding out to their place right now to arrest them and WJ wouldn't have ended up having a bent nose for the rest of his life. I'm disappointed in you, Brannigan.'

'I'm sorry, Marshal,' said Carl, even though he didn't really regret discovering the bank robbery money and arresting the Collins brothers.

'Sorry just isn't good enough. Now get out of my sight. You best come by in the morning and I'll tell you whether you still have a job.'

Carl headed for the doorway after he'd said, 'I'll see you later, WJ. I'm going to buy a horse and ride out and bury the grey.'

Marshal Dodds waited until Carl had left the office before he asked, 'What happened to his horse?'

WJ explained that someone had taken a shot at Carl when he was on his way back from searching the Collins's cabin and hit his horse and that's why he wasn't back when things started to get rough in the saloon.

'So he would have been back but for the son of a bitch taking a shot at him. Did he get a look at who it was?'

WJ shook his head and said, 'No, but he thinks it might be Vincent Henshall because he still blames Carl for his brother Mark's death.'

'If it was Vincent then it's probably got more to do with Brannigan seeing Shelley Morgan than revenge for his brother's death.'

WJ looked towards the door and said, 'He's a sneaky one. We were talking about Shelley earlier and he didn't say a word.'

'Take my advice, WJ, and stick with the saloon girls. They may not come cheap, but you can have a different one whenever you feel like it and they don't nag or make demands on you like wives or girlfriends do. Just make sure that you only go with the clean ones. You won't catch anything that'll make you scratch if you stick with Margo's girls.'

14

WJ had only stayed home long enough to change his clothes last night and then headed back into town. He'd said that the marshal had given him some advice about women and he intended to spend the night with Gloria who was one of Margo's girls. The marshal had figured it would be a good idea for WJ to have a saloon girl while his wounds were still showing, because Gloria would be full of sympathy and she would see him as some sort of hero. So Carl was alone when he made the short ride from WJ's cabin on the edge of town to the marshal's office. He'd spent a restless night wondering what the marshal's decision would be. He had mixed feelings about staying in Maple, especially after his conversation with William Morgan late yesterday. William Morgan had heard that someone had taken a shot at Carl and he was concerned that Shelley might be in danger if she was with Carl.

Carl had developed some strong feelings for Shelley, but he could understand that her pa must be terrified at the prospect of losing his remaining daughter. So perhaps the marshal might make things easy for him by taking away his badge and then he would have no reason to stay in Maple. Rebuilding his ranch-house wasn't an option because he didn't have the money for materials and there was also the possibility that it would be burned down again while the maniac was on the loose. He had thought of confronting Vincent Henshall, but without any proof he could do nothing except threaten him. And Vincent wasn't the only one who might want to destroy anything associated with the name of Brannigan. It seemed that there were still some folks who figured that Henry Morgan was involved in the robbery and had shot little Lucy Morgan, so perhaps Bryn Morgan's account of what happened hadn't reached everyone yet.

Carl tied the reins of the newly acquired sable mare to the hitch rail outside the marshal's office. He looked in the direction of Margo's saloon and smiled. He would miss WJ. They'd become good buddies. Perhaps WJ would end up with a girl like Shelley and settle down in another job which was less dangerous. He would probably be safe while Marshal Dodds was around, but Dodds wouldn't always be the marshal. Judging by recent events it seemed that being a lawman was going to become more and more dangerous.

The darkened office puzzled Carl. Perhaps the marshal was sleeping in after his long ride yesterday and had expected WJ to be here to see to the men in the cells. Carl opened the shutters and saw the overturned chairs and the papers scattered on the floor. The rifle case had been smashed and two weapons were missing.

'Is that you, WJ?' called out the voice from the cells. It was Marshal Dodds, but he sounded different. Carl hurried to the cells, wincing as the smell from the urinal pots reached his nostrils. All the cell doors were open, except for the one which Marshal Dodds was supporting himself against the bars. There was a long line of dried blood that stretched from the gaping wound on the side of his head down to his neck.

'Brannigan, get the spare keys from under my desk and let me out of this piss hole.'

'I'm not a cripple,' barked Dodds, after Carl had opened the cell door and tried to help him towards his desk.

'I'll go and get Doc Aubrey.'

'No you won't,' roared the marshal, and then ordered Carl to fetch him the water bowl and get the stove going to brew some coffee.

Carl asked what had happened as he watched the dried blood turn to liquid, causing extra red coloured streaks to run down the marshal's face as he washed it.

'One of those bastard Collins brothers hit me with a piss pot when I'd gone to empty it. I must have been tired after the ride yesterday and they caught me off guard. I don't know how long I lay in their piss. I started hollering, but I guess by then nobody was about. My head hurts like hell and I've been drifting in and out of sleep or unconsciousness, but I'm not sure which it was. I thought WJ would have been here by now.'

'He took your advice and spent the night with a saloon girl.'

Despite his discomfort the marshal managed a smile and said, 'That boy believes every word I say. I was only joking. Anyway, I've decided to keep you on, and you'll be my second in command, so to speak. WJ's heart is in the right place, but I don't think he's cut out to be in charge. But if you ever ignore my orders again you'll be out on your ear.'

Carl wanted to say that he'd decided to move on. A sort of thanks, but no thanks reply was what he had in mind, but he didn't say so.

'Marshal, why don't you let me get the doc? That gash looks nasty.'

'I'm all right,' replied the marshal who had calmed down. 'I'll have a mug of coffee and then I'll go and change my clothes, have me a bite of breakfast and then I'm going after those two bastards.'

'I'll go and get WJ and then I can come with you. I want to be there when they tell us who the man on the roof was.'

'You best stay here, Brannigan. I have a good idea where the dumb fools might have headed and I want to bring them in. You and WJ can tidy this place up and have a cell ready because I plan to bring them in by nightfall. I'm not the sensitive sort, but I'd rather you keep what happened to me quiet. I don't want to have to bang some heads together if I hear folks sniggering about the Collins's escape.'

'Sure thing, Marshal. I take it they didn't confess last night!'

'They told me a load of bull about you lying about finding the bank sack out at their place. They said an old uncle had visited them recently and given them the money that they used to buy the horses and some other things. Of course they were lying through their teeth, but it doesn't matter now because they'll end up swinging from a rope for attacking me and escaping from here. But don't worry; I'll make sure that one of them tells me who killed your pa and little Lucy.'

*   *   *

The marshal had left the office less than an hour ago and Carl had cleaned the place by the time that WJ appeared with a big grin on his face and asked, 'Does this mean the marshal's keeping you on? I saw him riding out of town when I was on my way to get changed.

Where's he off to?'

'Questions, questions,' replied Carl. 'Yes, he's keeping me on, but I have no idea where he's heading. All being well he'll be back before dark. I've been flogging away here, so why don't you go and check on our guests.'

Carl had counted, 'One, two, three, four, five,' before he heard WJ cry out, 'Holy shit,' and then come hurrying back to the main office area.

'What's happened to the prisoners? Have the Collins boys been moved for their own protection?'

'They haven't been moved anywhere, WJ. You'd better grab a seat and I'll tell you what happened, but first, how did your night go with Gloria?'

'I ain't a blabber mouth, especially with her being a lady. She told me that when she's saved up enough money she's going to leave Margo's and get a proper job. That's if she don't meet someone she can settle down with. Now are you going to tell me what's happened to the prisoners?'

'You're kidding me, aren't you?' was WJ's response when Carl had explained everything to him. 'Holy shit, I wouldn't want to be in their boots when he catches up with them. They'll wish they were dead already! What do you think he'll do to them?'

'He'll do like he said and bring them in for trial. The marshal lives by the law. He might rough them up a little if they give him any back chat, but that's all he'll do.'

'I guess you're right. And, buddy, I'm glad you kept your job.'

'So am I, WJ, but I've got something to tell you about my job which makes me feel a bit uneasy.'

Carl told WJ that the marshal wanted him to be his senior deputy, his second in command.

'Well I guess you're that already, Carl. I've no hard feelings about that.'

'I wouldn't have taken it if it upset you, WJ. Anyway, let's go and have a stroll around town. We haven't got any prisoners to worry about and the marshal won't be back for quite a while yet.'

* * *

WJ had been sent home early by Carl and was sound asleep when he was awakened by someone in the room. He slowly opened his eyes and reached for the gun beside his bed and called out in a sleepy voice, 'Who is it?'

'It's me, you big dope,' answered Carl as he made his way across the darkened room to his bed.

'Jesus, Carl, I thought you were a robber. Where've you been?'

'I decided to wait to see if the marshal might make it back. He turned up about half an hour ago and I had a mug of coffee with him.'

'What about the Collins boys?' WJ asked.

'The marshal wants us both to report in tomorrow by nine at the latest. He said he would tell us together, but he didn't bring them back like he promised.'

Carl undressed quickly and snuggled into the bed across the room from WJ's and then called out, 'Goodnight, WJ. It's been a long day and I had trouble sleeping last night.'

'That's funny, so did I,' replied WJ, thinking of Gloria.

15

WJ was still annoyed with Carl when they rode their horses down Main Street towards the marshal's office ready for their meeting with Marshal Dodds.

'He must have told you something about what happened when he caught up with the Collins brothers.'

'I've told you, WJ. He just said make sure we got in by nine o'clock and he'd tell us both at the same time. Remember it was late and I just wanted to get to my bed. Anyway, we're here now and so is the marshal. I bet that poor horse of his didn't fancy being up early either.'

The marshal was seated at his desk and he lifted the large gold watch from his waistcoat pocket and said, 'Good, you're both on time. Now the first thing you need to know is that the brothers are dead and buried.'

'You mean someone had killed them before you caught up with them?' asked a surprised WJ.

'No, WJ. I found them both alive and they wouldn't give themselves up so I ended up shooting them. It'll save a trial. They had some money on them, but although it wasn't much I suppose it'll have to be returned to the bank.'

'Jesus,' was all that WJ said.

Carl was about to ask a question when the marshal suggested that the deputies went and got some breakfast over at the café. He would fill them in on the details later.

Carl and WJ discussed the marshal's dramatic news that he'd killed the brothers in between mouthfuls of beans and eggs. They had both been surprised that the Collins brothers would have resisted arrest if the marshal had them pinned down somewhere. Carl was thinking how easily they gave themselves up to him when he arrested them in the saloon.

'Carl, do you think the marshal never caught up with the boys and he's lied about killing them?'

'It's possible. His pride was certainly hurt when they escaped. He might think that the brothers will never come back here so no one will ever find out that they're not dead.'

*   *   *

When Carl and WJ returned to the office the marshal seemed in a relaxed mood and ready to give them the details. He didn't flinch when Carl mentioned about being surprised that they didn't give themselves up.

'I figure that the brothers decided they would rather risk dying from a bullet than face the hanging that would have awaited them,' suggested the marshal. 'Perhaps they thought they would get the better of me for a second time. I don't know, but it was their choice. Now let me tell you what they told me before I shot them. They

153

answered the questions I shouted to them, which surprised me, but perhaps they were playing for time. I had them pinned down where they'd stopped for the night.'

'Did they admit doing the robbery,' WJ asked impatiently.

'They boasted about it, so Bryn Morgan was right all along about them being the two who entered the bank.'

'What about the man on the roof? Did he kill the girl?' Carl asked.

The marshal nodded and then paused before he said, 'And he also killed your pa.'

WJ and Carl asked the question at the same time, 'But why?'

'It was Arnie who said the man knew that your pa had recognized him in the alleyway after he had come down off the roof. For what its worth I believe what the boys told me, before they started shooting at me.'

'So you know who killed Pa?' Carl asked, ready to drop his suspicions about whether the marshal was lying about killing the brothers.

'I'm sorry, Brannigan, I'm going to have to disappoint you there. Arnie was probably dead before he hit the ground, but his brother lingered a while. He was trying to tell me something when he took his dying breath, but we'll never know what it was. I guess you must be disappointed.'

Carl told the marshal that it wasn't his fault that they still didn't know the identity of the man on the roof, but the marshal still expressed his guilt. 'Well, I do blame myself for letting them escape in the first place.'

Carl was still a mite suspicious and asked, 'So where did you catch up with them and what town are they buried in?'

'It was about ten miles this side of Garcia Town and that's where I buried them. I figured they had no kin that we know of and just thought it would be easier to bury them on the spot near where they died. I was lucky that a feller came by in a wagon and he had a shovel.'

Carl had another question, but he planned to ask it later.

'So now you both know as much as I do. Maybe one day the mystery man might slip up and he'll face a hanging. I have a feeling that things are about to get quieter around here, so I was thinking of going to stay with my sister and her family for a few weeks. That's if you two can cope without me again.'

WJ felt his nose, remembering the last time, but he and Carl agreed that they could handle things.

'Good, I've got a few matters to attend to before I go so I'll be around for the next couple of days.'

* * *

It was nearly noon when Carl returned from doing his rounds and was surprised to find the marshal in the office, because he was meant to have left for his vacation by now.

'I had a bit of last minute paperwork to do,' said the marshal and then added: 'I'm just off to the café to have something to eat, but I'll call in here before I head off in case there's something you've forgotten to ask me about. I know you'll do a good job while I'm away and keep an eye on WJ.'

Carl waited for a few minutes after the marshal had left before he settled himself into his boss's chair and put his feet up on the desk. He wanted to be in that position when WJ came in so that he could tease him by ordering him to clean out the cells. He saw the marshal's badge on the table and he reached for it intending to pin it on his shirt in place of his deputy's badge and see if WJ noticed, but he left the badge where it was when he spotted the keys next to it.

Carl hesitated for a moment and fingered the keys that included the one to the office safe. What he had in mind was deceitful. The marshal had been good to him and snooping amongst his private belongings wasn't the way to repay him. Then he got to thinking that it wasn't the marshal's private safe. It was for official business and so there shouldn't be anything in there that he wasn't supposed to see and if the marshal hadn't been so cagey about it then there would be no need to be curious.

The marshal usually took his time when he visited the café because he believed that eating should be like making love and not be rushed. Carl and WJ had been amused by that remark because the only woman that the marshal had been with to their knowledge, was Margo. Any nurturing he did with Margo would have cost him extra because she charged strictly by the hour, and the marshal wasn't renowned for parting with his money.

Carl had no idea which key fitted the safe and he'd tried most of them before he heard the lock click and he was able to ease the door open. He removed the contents and placed them on the desk in the order they had been removed so that he could return them without raising the marshal's suspicion. He was beginning to think that his curiosity was in vain when he reached towards the back of the safe and his hand touched a small sack. He struggled to remove it because it must have been squeezed into the safe. Carl undid the cord of the familiar Maple Bank sack and had withdrawn one of the thick wads of dollar bills when the door opened and Marshal Dodds came in.

Carl had the sack in one hand and the notes in the other when the marshal drew his gun and said, 'Well it's a damn shame, Brannigan, that you let your curiosity get the better of you. I could say that I was holding that money for safe keeping, but I don't think you'd believe me. I could ask you to forget what you've seen here and I could give you a cut, but I expect you'd refuse, just like your stupid old pa did.'

'But my pa had nothing to do with the robbery, everyone knows that,' said Carl still shocked by what he'd found, and now it was clear that the marshal

159

had been involved in the robbery.

'Of course he didn't,' Dodds agreed, 'except that he saw me in the alleyway after I'd come off the roof and removed the neckerchief from my face. I offered to pay him to keep his mouth shut, but he refused. So I hung him and made it look like suicide.'

'You bastard!' Carl shouted and debated going for his gun, even though the marshal had the advantage.

'That little girl's death was an accident. I just fired a few shots to stop anyone from playing the hero and she ran out from nowhere. When you turned up to report your pa's death, I was thinking that you'd found out that I was involved.'

'So you let the Collins brothers escape and went after them and killed them to make sure they didn't reveal your identity?'

'Exactly right. Arnie was supposed to give me a tap on the head just to make sure there was some blood so it would look as though I'd been attacked during their escape. The silly bastard whacked me so hard he nearly killed me. If the Collins brothers had done as they were told and not flashed their money about they'd still be alive.'

'So what happens now, Marshal?'

Dodds laughed and said, 'What happens now is that I'm going to kill you.'

'You won't get away with this, Marshal.'

'I think I will. After I've killed you I'll shoot that feller you put in the cells last night and say I came back and found you dead and the prisoner about to escape so I shot him. You should have kept your . . . '

The marshal was interrupted by the door being pushed open and it distracted him long enough for Carl to drop the money from his hand, draw his pistol and fire at the marshal. The first bullet thudded into his body. The second that splattered the left side of the marshal's temple was fired in anger and revenge for his father. Carl had decided that he wouldn't risk a weak jury finding Dodds not guilty.

'What the hell's happening!' shouted WJ as he forced the door open and stepped over the marshal's body.

'He deserved it, WJ. You just saved my life. If you hadn't opened that door when you did then I would have been dead by now.'

'You've killed the marshal, Carl. I'll ask you again what the hell happened here. And why is all that money on the floor? I've never seen so many dollar bills in one place before.'

'It's a long story, WJ, and it's going to take some believing. I'll tell you everything when I get back from seeing the mayor, but we need to put the marshal's body in one of the empty cells before somebody comes investigating the gunfire. Best lock the door from the inside.'

⋆ ⋆ ⋆

Mayor Jefferson shuffled some papers as he waited for the town council to settle in their seats in the community hall. In addition to the town council he had invited William and Bryn Morgan to the hastily arranged meeting. Some of the members were annoyed that they had been summoned without any explanation. There were mutterings as they watched Carl and WJ take a seat alongside the mayor who was seated behind the long table.

Mayor Jefferson stood up and cleared his throat, something he always did when he was about to speak at such a gathering.

'Gentlemen, I have to tell you that Marshal Dodds is dead and is at this moment being prepared for burial by Stanley Beaumont. As far as we know he had no kinfolk close by and I propose that he will be buried in a secret location and not in the town's cemetery.'

Everyone present except those on the mayor's table turned and looked at the person next to them. There were more mutterings, some of them loud this time.

'Marshal Dodds was shot by Deputy Brannigan in his office less than half an hour ago. You will be pleased to know that a good deal of the bank robbery money has now been recovered. Marshal Dodds was an accomplice of the Collins brothers.' The mayor paused and some of the shocked gathering looked sympathetically towards William and Bryn Morgan.

The mayor cleared his throat again and continued. 'Dodds admitted to being the man who hanged Henry Brannigan to make it look like suicide so that Henry would be blamed for Lucy's death. He feared that Henry might have recognized him as the infamous man on the roof. I am sorry to present you with the stark details, but Deputy Brannigan will now tell you an incredible story of deceit and murder. I have asked Carl Brannigan to become the new marshal of Maple and we must all hope that he accepts.' The audience were spellbound as the mayor invited Carl to explain the extraordinary background to the sequence of events.

Carl was a bit overawed by the audience. He had never made a speech or presentation in his life, but he did it well. He only faltered when he explained how and why Marshal Dodds confessed to being the man who had murdered his father and shot little Lucy. He sat down after delivering his story and was embarrassed by the loud applause from the gathering, just as he was later when there was much back slapping and handshaking. WJ just kept grinning when Carl introduced him. Carl had told the meeting that if WJ had not come into the marshal's office at that critical moment then the evil marshal would still be alive, and he'd be dead. The warmest handshakes and heartfelt thanks came from Bryn and William Morgan, who said that Carl would be welcome if he wanted to come calling on his daughter, Shelley.

16

Carl took the marshal's job and it was a couple of months before people accepted him as a mere mortal and not some kind of hero. He knew that things might get back to normal when during yesterday's tour of Margo's Saloon she'd moaned about the patrols not being frequent enough. He'd promised to speak to the town council about an extra deputy. Life was good, but he was about to receive an unexpected setback when he called on William Morgan.

He should have sensed something was wrong by the grave expression on William Morgan's face and the redness around Shelley's eyes. Perhaps it was because the Morgans were devout churchgoers and he was about to be given the answer to a question he'd asked yesterday and been told to wait while it was considered.

'Carl, you will know that no one has greater respect for you than this family,' William Morgan began, and then continued in a serious tone, 'You eased our pain in a way that we could never describe. The Bible tells us not to be vengeful and maybe it was wrong to rejoice in the death of Lucy's killer, but we did. So it is with a heavy heart that I must refuse to give you Shelley's hand in marriage.' Carl looked towards Shelley and saw the fresh tears flowing as William Morgan started to offer his reasons.

'Yours is a dangerous job and likely to become more so. Some folks tell me that your reputation will spread and there will be men who will come here to challenge you in the hope that they will become famous if they kill you. Shelley would face a life of wondering if a new day would bring a fresh danger for you. She would fear that she might lose a loving husband and if God blessed her with your children, they would be deprived of their father. We can only hope that you will understand.'

Carl could understand even though it had come as a surprise. He looked towards Shelley and she looked as sad as he'd ever seen anyone, even at a funeral.

Carl hoped he had a solution when he asked, 'And what if I gave up being marshal? There would be no gain for a gunslinger shooting a farmer or a rancher which is what I would become.'

William Morgan looked towards his daughter whose face had brightened by what had just been said and then he faced Carl again and replied, 'But you would be making a sacrifice that you may regret later and in time you might blame this family for making you do it and that would hurt Shelley.'

'Mister Morgan, I love Shelley and I will make that sacrifice and I swear on my pa's memory that I will never hold it against your family.'

There was an agonizing silence for Shelley and Carl until William Morgan gave his decision. 'Then you have my permission to marry my daughter,' he said with a smile. Shelley was about to shriek out with joy when her daddy added, 'but there is one condition.' He paused as though teasing them and then continued. 'You must be willing to accept a sizable sum of money to rebuild and restock your ranch.'

'I will,' said Carl just before Shelley hugged him, then her daddy, mom and finally uncle Bryn. As soon as the kissing and tears had stopped, it was Bryn Morgan's turn to spring a surprise. He announced that he had abandoned his plans to become a minister and was thinking of buying the Henshall ranch.

Everyone laughed when he turned to Carl and jokingly said that he would have to decide what rate he would charge for water and grazing rights.

* * *

Carl was working the last week of his notice when the new marshal arrived.

Jack Burrows came with a good reputation and Carl was confident that he would take care of WJ. He'd also brought a deputy of his own so Margo could stop moaning about her saloon not being patrolled enough. Carl was impressed how Burrows went about reorganizing things in the office, including clearing out lots of old paperwork.

* * *

It was during Carl's last day as a lawman when Marshal Burrows revealed some disturbing news. 'You ought to read this letter, Carl. It was amongst the papers in the back room that I've been going through as part of my clear out.'

The letter was from Marshal Took in Bugle Falls asking Marshal Dodds to warn Carl that Kelvin Gains, the father of the man he'd had to shoot, had confessed to hiring two men to kill Carl. Gains had tried to call them off, but he feared that they still planned to do it.

As Carl put the letter back on the

desk Burrows handed him a 'Wanted Poster' and said, 'That was attached to the letter and I guess it's a description of one of the men, although the letter doesn't make that clear, and it's not dated.'

Carl didn't need to study the sketch of the man. He knew who he was.

'I don't need to worry about this one, Marshal, because I had to kill him over at Margo's a while back. There can't be two men that ugly with such spooky eyes.'

'And what about his partner?' Burrows asked.

'I don't think he had one. If he did then he didn't show up at the burial of the troublemaker.'

'So how did you come to kill Mister Ugly?'

Carl explained about the incident over at Margo's and how he'd been sent for because there was trouble brewing.

'Perhaps that was a setup to get you over there,' said Burrows. 'Let's hope the other feller mentioned in the letter gave up the idea of killing you.'

* * *

The rider looked up at the bunting strung across Main Street. He smiled when he read the large letters 'Good Luck Marshal Brannigan'. He hadn't planned to come back to Maple Town, but now he was glad he had. He wondered if the saloon girl with the missing tooth was still here and where his stupid ex-partner was buried. Kyle Mason had messed up his plans, but he had taken a contract and he aimed to see it through. Joe Harper regarded himself as a professional. He would finish the job and he would do it today, and then he would go and collect his money, even though he should have done so months ago. At least now he would be able to have Kyle's share and Brannigan had saved him the job of killing Kyle. 'Good Luck Marshal Brannigan,' he said to himself as he dismounted outside Margo's. Perhaps Brannigan was leaving and that's what the message meant. Well he'd be leaving in a wooden box. There would be no staying in a hotel this time, he just needed the cover of darkness and he would get it over with and be gone.

The bar was quiet and Harper bought a beer and settled in a seat out of the way. He could have waited outside of town, but it would be dark within a couple of hours and he could while away the time until then. He'd have a few beers, maybe visit the café, but maybe not, he thought, remembering Kyle's belly ache after their visit there.

Harper had been running through a few ideas of what he would do with the second instalment for the job and he was surprised when Margo settled in the seat next to his, blew smoke in the air and asked him if he was looking for company.

'I might be,' he replied and gave her a flashing smile.

'You're cute, mister. We don't get many like you in here. And I guess you must be horny to be looking for it at this time of day and when you're sober. What's your name, stranger?'

'The girls call me Greedy,' he said.

'Cheeky with it as well. So, Greedy, what do you want exactly?'

'Is Joanne available?' Harper asked, remembering her shapely body.

'Sorry, she left us a few weeks ago and went back to some God-forsaken town in Nevada. She got fed up with all those cruel remarks about her missing tooth.'

'That's a pity,' said a disappointed Harper.

Margo moved closer to Harper and said, 'I think you might have misunderstood my question. I meant do what you want to do with me. The girls don't start work for another couple of hours. I'm the only one here during the day and I charge a special rate which is half of what you would have paid Joanne.'

'I tell you what, sweetheart,' said Harper. 'Arrange to have a couple of beef sandwiches sent up to your room for me after we've had ourselves some

174

real pleasure and we have a deal.'

'You drive a hard bargain, cowboy. It's a deal, but you'd better not disappoint me. I don't do this thing just for the money.'

As Margo led the way towards the stairs she asked the barmen to arrange to have the sandwiches sent up in an hour.

Joe didn't really care what a woman looked like as long as she knew how to give a man pleasure and she let him know that he was giving her the same. He couldn't abide women who made love with their mouth closed and stayed still until it was over. Margo undressed and climbed on top of him, her face reddened and he could see by her eyes that she'd meant that she didn't do it just for the money. He smelt the tobacco on her breath as she forced her tongue inside his mouth. He had intended on removing his clothes, but he had only undone his shirt and pushed his trousers to his knees by the time their flesh had been joined. Margo was certainly noisy as she rode on top of him, but he suspected that most of her breathlessness was because she was out of condition rather than being the sound of passion. But as they climaxed there was no doubting that her cries were genuine when he felt the blast of her hot breath in his face.

* * *

Joe felt her nudge him in the ribs and then he heard the knock on the door that signalled the arrival of the sand-wiches. A quick look at the darkness outside told him that the barman hadn't followed Margo's instructions because they'd been in the room for much longer than an hour.

Margo looked disappointed as Harper struggled to dress himself and it became clear that he was leaving.

'You don't have to go,' she said and tapped the bed, inviting him to rejoin her.

'I'm afraid I do, but maybe another

time,' he replied.

He hurried down the stairs that led to the bar which was now heaving with cowboys. One laughed at him as he passed by when he saw Harper was fastening the buckle on his belt. His shirt buttons were undone, making it clear where he'd been.

Harper rushed out into the street, feeling annoyed that he might have messed things up, but luck was on his side because he spotted Brannigan passing by a lantern on the opposite sidewalk He was carrying what looked like some parcels and he was heading up Main Street to the quiet part of town.

A passer-by shouted out, 'It's your last night of freedom, Carl. Enjoy your wedding tomorrow.'

Harper pulled out his pistol and crossed the street and climbed on to the sidewalk on the same side of the street as Brannigan. He had already selected the spot where he would fire from and was within a few feet of reaching it, his gun pointing at Brannigan's back, when he heard the voice behind him shout, 'Drop your weapon or you're dead!'

Harper reeled around still holding his gun. He couldn't get a clear view of the caller, but saw the flash as the gun was fired twice, sending him sprawling off the sidewalk and into the dusty street.

Brannigan had dropped the presents he'd been given by some of the towns-folk and drawn his gun, but he would have been dead by now had it not been for WJ who was checking on the dead Harper.

WJ approached Carl and started helping him pick up the wedding presents, when Carl said, 'I guess I owe you big time, buddy. Do you know who that feller is and why were you following him or were you following me?'

'I don't now what they call him, but that son of a bitch used to be the part-ner of the feller you killed in Margo's. You know, the one who used the broken glass on that feller who he accused of staring at him.'

'How do you know?'

'I was in the office this afternoon when Marshal Burrows mentioned the warning from your old marshal at Bugle Falls. Marshal Burrows showed me the wanted poster and told me that you identified him as the feller that you'd shot in Margo's. Well I recognized him as well and I also remembered the feller I'd seen him with him and that's him there. I almost bumped into them in the doorway of Margo's and I guess their faces just stuck in my mind when I saw them both later. I saw him ride into town this afternoon, and decided to keep an eye on him and that's why I followed him.'

'Thanks, buddy. I guess you've got some paperwork to do and will be passing some business to Mr Beaumont. I hope you won't be late for my wedding tomorrow.'

As WJ walked away Carl shook his head when he realized how close he'd come to dying on his last day as a law man and the day before he was getting married.

17

Carl had drifted back to sleep after he had mused about the life ahead of him with his new wife. He hadn't liked the idea of accepting William Morgan's offer of money to rebuild his ranch, but he was insistent. Some folks had told him that it was normal for the bride's family to give their daughter a generous gift and William Morgan could certainly afford it. Carl had discovered that the Morgan family had business interests in other towns, including a number of general stores. They also owned property and businesses back East bought from Kathryn Morgan's inheritance and expanded by the shrewdness of Bryn Morgan. They'd settled in Maple because Kathryn Morgan fell in love with the place while they were passing through and ran the store because it was what William had always wanted to do.

Carl was looking forward to restoring the ranch to what it was like during his happiest days there. He had plans to dig out a feed from the river so that he could have his own independent water supply and he had other ideas. It would all take time, but he was young and he was building for the future and the children he hoped that Shelley would bear him. He'd smiled at the thought of becoming a dad one day, God willing.

He thought he was dreaming that some no-good was kicking and shaking him, until he recognized WJ's voice.

'Carl, get up. You've got to come quick.' WJ yelled for the second time.

'Very funny, WJ. I know, you're going to tell me that I've slept in and I'm late for my wedding.'

'No, you're not late, but the marshal told me to fetch you. He wouldn't tell me what it was about, but he looked really worried.'

Carl threw back the bed covering and started to climb out of bed, but stopped after he'd checked his watch which was on a table nearby and said, 'Hang on, WJ, I don't work for the marshal anymore. I'm going to get some coffee brewing and make me some breakfast. You tell the marshal that I'll see him later before I head back here and get togged up for my wedding. By the way I hope you're not planning to come to my wedding in those old clothes.'

'Carl, I swear on my folks' memory I ain't kidding with you. The marshal sounded real serious and William Morgan was with him.'

Carl sprang up from the bed and shouted, 'Why didn't you tell me it was about the Morgans. It must be something to do with the wedding. WJ, you best saddle my horse while I get dressed.'

★ ★ ★

Carl dismounted outside the marshal's office and left WJ to tether his horse, but before he rushed towards the steps that led to the sidewalk he'd threatened to make WJ's life hell if this was a prank.

Any thought of pranks disappeared from his mind when he saw the grim look on the faces of William Morgan and Marshal Burrows.

'Carl, Mister Morgan called in to report that he's very concerned because Shelley hasn't returned from her morning ride.'

'How late is she?' Carl asked as he sensed that something was seriously wrong.

'Over an hour, but she's never been late before,' replied William Morgan. 'She should have been back on time knowing there were things to be done today, and she needed to help her mother.'

'Maybe her horse just went lame and she's decided to stay with the animal knowing we'd come looking for her, or she might have had to walk. Me and WJ will go looking for her now. There are only two routes she would have taken, so one of us will find her. Tell her mom that if it's me that finds Shelley then I'll close my eyes and we can call to each other from a distance. I know how superstitious Mrs Morgan is about the bride and groom not seeing each other until they are in church.'

When they were outside Carl explained his plan to WJ and they were soon mounted and heeling their horses into a gallop along Main Street.

They'd reached the fork in the trail when Carl signalled for WJ to head straight on while he followed the trail that led to the Grove Hills where he'd taken Shelley on their first ride together. As he rode he was greatly concerned that she might have come to some harm, but hoping that perhaps she had just panicked about the marriage. She was only eighteen and the thought of becoming a wife at such a young age might have suddenly hit her. Perhaps she was sitting somewhere now trying to decide what to do.

Carl passed the yew tree where they had visited many times and rode to the spot where he'd looked down to the river below and explained some of the landmarks. He surveyed the deserted area and realized that his hunch was wrong. He would head back to town and hope that she had returned on her own or that WJ had found her. She would be embarrassed, but it would all be forgotten by the time they were married in a few hours from now.

Carl was in for his first disappointment when he approached the joining of the two trails and saw WJ. He was alone and looked solemn as he shook his head. WJ told him that he'd spoken to a family who were part of a small wagon train and had been camped near the trail. They'd been up since dawn, but hadn't seen Shelley, only two men riding towards town, but they couldn't describe them except to say that they just looked ordinary. The men had been riding fine looking horses and according to one of the men from the wagons the fancy looking saddles must have cost a lot of bucks.

'Let's head back for town, WJ,' said Carl and heeled his horse to start the gallop home.

'I'm sure she'll be all right, buddy,' said WJ hopefully.

Carl didn't share WJ's optimism. The mention of two men riding into town had reminded him of another two men, the Collins brothers. He had never been totally convinced about Marshall Dodds claim about killing the brothers. Now he was remembering the threat against Shelley that Ike Collins had made when he'd arrested them. What if they were still alive and they'd come back to seek their revenge for their dog, Killerboy! Surely no one would do such a thing, but Carl remembered the tears in Ike's eyes when he spoke of his dog. The only consolation he could hang on to was that the brothers could never be described as ordinary, which is what the folks in the wagons had said about the two riders. But he still remembered the two horses and saddles the Collins brothers had bought with the bank robbery money.

Carl told WJ he would see him back at the marshal's office and pulled up his horse outside the Morgan's store. Kathryn Morgan's tear stained face told him that Shelley hadn't come home and there were more tears when he told them that he and WJ hadn't found her. He tried to console them by going through the various possibilities that Shelley was safe and that everything was going to be all right. But they didn't seem comforted by the time he left to continue his search. William Morgan followed Carl outside and told him something that had him eager to check in on the marshal's office. Then he was going to pay a call on the son of a bitch who he had just been told had been pestering Shelley.

Marshal Burrows was talking to WJ when Carl entered the office and he told Carl that it was time to get together some men and organize a search party.

'It sounds like a good idea, Marshal, but I need to go and see someone first.

I've just been told that he's been pestering Shelley these past few weeks. Maybe he's kidnapped her because she was planning to get married today.'

WJ was about to suggest who it might be, but he would have been wrong when Carl revealed that it was Daniel Jefferson.

'Isn't he the mayor's son?' asked Burrows who'd only met him once.

'He's only a kid,' added WJ without answering the marshal's question.

'He's not much younger than Shelley, but kid or no kid he's been pestering her,' Carl said with anger in his voice and then explained, 'According to William Morgan the little son of a bitch has been following her when she's been out riding. He says he's harmless, but I'm not so sure. I saved him from a beating once, but I'll give him one if he's done anything to harm Shelley.'

Carl headed towards the door, but halted when the marshal called after him. 'Now hold on, Carl. You're too riled to go questioning this boy. You might frighten him into silence. I'll handle this. Don't add to your troubles by forcing me to lock you up.'

Carl knew that the marshal was right and sat down, but he was soon pacing up and down the office.

'The marshal should be back by now,' he snapped at WJ.

Carl was on the point of going to the mayor's house on the edge of town when a grim faced marshal came through the door.

'Did you talk to the kid?' Carl asked angrily.

'No. He wasn't there. It seems he went riding early this morning and he hasn't come back. His father was about to go looking for him. It's too much of a coincidence, so we ought to get moving! I've got half a dozen men outside ready to join the search party.'

Carl headed for the door, brushing aside the marshal after he said that it might be best if Carl stayed in town and waited for some news.

The party split into two groups of

four after Carl had insisted that he had his own plans and rode off. The marshal had let WJ work out the areas to search and when the party reached the end of Main Street the groups headed off in different directions with the marshal leading one group and WJ the other. The men had been told to fire two shots into the air if they found anything to report.

Carl knew that he might be wasting his time by heading for the Henshall ranch-house, but it would make the perfect hiding place. Vincent Henshall hadn't been seen for weeks and it seemed that he had fled because of his debts. It was likely that Daniel Jefferson would have heard his father talking about the downfall of Vincent and know that the house was unoccupied.

★　★　★

He saw the Henshall ranch-house in the distance and he felt the hairs on the back of his neck rise and a shiver pass over his body when he sensed that his hunch was correct. It was what Marshal Took had said all good lawmen develop with experience. He had thought the old marshal was spinning him a yarn at the time, but now he was urging his horse into a full gallop.

The Henshall Ranch had been one of the finest in the territory and Carl had once been a regular visitor. He saw the clump of trees to the right of the trail that led to the big house. It was the trees that he'd played in with Mark when they were boys and chased some of the girls who'd been invited to one of Mark's boyhood birthdays. Unlike his own folks, the Henshalls' had had a wide circle of friends. Some of them had been involved in business and others in politics. When Mark and Carl had reached manhood Mark organized his own parties. There had never been any shortage of girls from out of town. Some of them had been wild and daring and so different to the girls he'd grown up with. There was something scheming about the girls who made it clear that they wanted Carl and Mark for fun, but had other plans for marriage. It suited them both because marriage had been the last thing on their minds, but things changed when Isobel Clayman blossomed into a woman. Unlike the snooty girls, she had made it clear that she wanted marriage and nothing was going to happen with any man until then. It wasn't just Mark and Carl whom she drove crazy. She had attracted the attention of Vincent as well which came as a surprise because he had always shown a preference for the more refined lady.

Carl pulled back on the reins when he heard the two shots in the distance just as he approached the house. He had ridden off before the marshal had given out the instruction to the search parties about firing to signal that someone had discovered something. Carl scanned the ranch-house and grounds as he drew closer. It was still spectacular, but there was no sign of life, or so he thought until he heard, and then saw the window at the top of house being opened. His attention was drawn away as he sensed movement to his right. A rider must have come galloping from the side of the house. Carl's instinct was to follow him as he saw him disappear through the trees and out of sight, but as he looked towards the window he saw a woman climbing out. There was no mistaking the long auburn curls. It was Shelley. He was mesmerized as she prepared to jump. She might have screamed, but he hadn't heard her above his own anguished cry and he watched her plunge, and then land with a sickening thud in front of the ranch house door. He almost crashed into Shelley as he dismounted while his horse was on the move and he was distraught as he slid the last few yards and came to rest beside his sweetheart. His eyes filled with tears when he saw her swollen and bloodied face. He pulled the torn dress across her exposed legs and placed his arm under head. Her eyelids lifted and he said, 'You're going to be all right, my love. I'll get you to Doc Aubrey.'

'I'm not dirty, am I?' she whispered. 'I love you, Carl. I would have loved you forever.'

'And I'll love you forever, my sweet innocent beauty,' he whispered back, his voice choked with emotion.

She didn't speak again and he cradled her long after he knew she had died, and so had part of him.

'I need to put you somewhere safe, my love,' he said as he lifted her gently and carried her inside the house and placed her on the large sofa. He looked around the room for something suitable to cover her before ripping down the rich velvet curtain and gently placed it over her body.

Once outside he mounted his horse, rubbed the tears from his eyes and pulled on the reins before he headed in the direction that he believed Daniel Jefferson was heading. He rode with a determination that he'd never shown

194

before. It was as though he was preparing to ride in a straight line from now and through the night, knowing that he would eventually catch the man he regarded as the lowest form of animal life. He had already decided that he would kill Jefferson and forget any notion of letting the law take care of him.

He didn't know what sort of start Shelley's kidnapper had or whether he might have left the trail. He started to blame himself as he'd done when his father died. He knew that Marshal Dodds would have killed his father whether or not Carl had come home, but it was different with Shelley. She would have married someone else and still be alive if she hadn't met Carl.

He pushed his guilty thoughts aside and recalled the image of Daniel Jefferson into his mind. He was thinking that if he didn't catch him today it wouldn't matter because there would be other days. There would be no hiding place for the man who had taken one dear life, and ruined others, including Brannigan's.

He felt the overhanging branches brush against his leg as the trail narrowed as it ran between a stretch of trees. He heard the sound of a rattling chain a fraction before he heard the growl that spooked his horse and sent him crashing to the ground. The dog circled around the horse as it prepared to attack him. It was thinner than the last time he'd seen it, but there was no mistaking that it was the Collins's dog. There could be no sparing its life this time. He drew his pistol and aimed it at the dog as it lunged towards him. The bullet hit the middle of its forehead and although it must have died instantly the momentum of the lunge caused it to land on top of him. He pushed it to one side and then inspected the blood-stained body. It hadn't registered with him until now just how close he was to the Collins's place.

The dog had obviously pulled the chain from its kennel and likely had been looking for food. Marshal Dodds had lied again when he'd claimed to have shot and buried the dog when he'd ridden out to search the Collins's cabin. Carl hadn't convinced the Collins brothers that he really hadn't killed the dog even though he had come close to it before he thought of an idea. He had used his rope to lasso the dog, and then pull it away from the kennel. He'd secured the rope around the tree so that it couldn't move more than three feet and reach him. He had searched the kennel and found the money bags from the bank under a loose floorboard. Before he left he'd untied the rope so that the dog could reach the pile of food that had been left near the kennel.

He took a little while to calm his horse, then remounted and urged it forward, but he was soon pulling on the reins and turning back to where he'd seen the dog emerging from the trees.

The Collins place could only be a short ride from here and he had to consider the possibility that Daniel Jefferson had gone there to hide. Carl couldn't afford to carry on the main trail and be left wondering if Jefferson was holed up in the Collins cabin so that was where he headed.

★　★　★

He pulled up his horse, tethered it to a tree a short distance from the cabin and made his way on foot. Something didn't seem right and now he was wondering how Daniel Jefferson could have released the dog. Carl was remembering what WJ had told him the people on the wagon train had seen the two riders on fine looking horses. Maybe Daniel Jefferson was just a lovesick kid and had nothing to do with Shelley's death? Perhaps Ike Collins had carried out his threat and that meant he and his brother couldn't be far from here. His mind was muddled as he reasoned that the brothers would have taken the chain off. He was trying to make sense as he drew close to the cabin and saw the familiar horse tethered to a rail.

He couldn't identify the sound. It alternated between a groan, and a gurgling noise. He drew his pistol and stepped into the open near the broken kennel. Carl had seen horrific injuries caused by broken bottles being rammed into a face, but nothing compared to this. The man was barely recognizable. The right side of his face no longer had an eye, cheek or ear because they had been ripped away. The opening where the mouth had been was now a gaping hole and only a few broken teeth remained. The gurgling sound was made by the blood that bubbled from the large wound in his throat as he struggled to breathe. One hand was unmarked while the other had just the thumb remaining. Patches of clothing had been torn away along with the flesh they had covered and the bloodiest area was between his legs. Carl had been right about having doubts about it being Daniel Jefferson, but it wasn't Ike or Arnie Collins either. Carl looked at the horse that he now realized was the one he'd seen being ridden away when he went to attend to Shelley. It was Vincent Henshall's horse, but it wasn't Vincent who was writhing in agony. It was Bryn Morgan. Carl didn't know how this monster of a man could have survived the attack by the dog, but he must be only minutes away from dying.

Carl's study of Morgan's disfigurement was disturbed by a rustling nearby. He turned and saw a group of rats. He figured there must have been six or more. He reached for some stones and was about to throw them at the rats when he saw Morgan's head turn in their direction. The single eye reacted to the advancing creatures. Carl walked in a wide circle and undid the reins of Henshall's horse and led it away from the cabin. As he passed by the kennel heading towards his own horse he shouted, 'Don't worry, Morgan, you'll soon be in hell.'

Carl doubted if his shout had been

heard, but he hoped it had because it might mean that Morgan could hear the advancing rats.

When Carl reached the spot where the dead dog lay he was glad that his plan during the search of the kennel for the bank robbery money had spared the dog's life. The dog must have broken loose some months ago, but stayed close to the cabin, perhaps out of loyalty to the Collins brothers who had rescued him. Carl was thinking that fate worked in strange ways at times.

18

Shelley had started her wedding day with her usual morning ride and she'd urged her horse, Blossom into a gallop as she left Main Street and joined the trail out of the eastern side of town. It was the same route that she'd taken every morning since her family had settled in Maple. She would normally be taking it again this afternoon, but not today. This was the day she hoped to cherish for the rest of her life. She was getting married to a man she loved dearly and knew he would make sure her days were filled with happiness. Her mother had questioned whether she had known him long enough, but Shelley had pointed out it had been about the same time that she had known Daddy before they married. Her mom had never mentioned it again. Shelley smiled to herself when she thought of her mother back home and probably getting into a panic. Daddy would calm her down, like he always did, and she knew that they were going to enjoy today as well.

When she saw the rider approaching her she felt excited. It was very early and the town was still asleep. It must be Carl. It would be just like him to ignore her mother's warning yesterday that it was bad luck to see the bride on their wedding day until they were in the church.

She was on the point of turning her horse off the trail and making him chase after her when she recognized Vincent Henshall's distinctive black stallion with a white diamond flash on its head. The rider wasn't Carl or Vincent. It was her Uncle Bryn.

As he drew close she could see him smile with satisfaction that he had surprised her.

Shelley's shoulders relaxed now that she knew that Vincent hadn't returned.

He was the last person she would want to see today.

'Uncle Bryn, I thought you were at the store. What are you doing riding Vincent's horse?'

'Because it's my horse. I knew you'd be surprised. The Henshall Ranch became mine two days' ago and this animal came with it. And I've got another surprise for you on your special day.'

'What is it?' she asked, thinking that it might be something connected with Carl's ranch.

'Hmm, I'm not sure that I should tell you now,' he teased.

'But you must, Uncle Bryn. You know I can never wait until Christmas to open my presents. Remember you caught me opening them once when I was a little girl.'

Bryn Morgan smiled when he told her that he remembered the occasion.

'All right,' he said with a sigh. 'It's a young foal that was sired by this beauty of mine. She's over at the

Henshall stables. Why don't we ride over there now and it'll be part of Blossom's exercise.'

Shelley faltered for a moment wondering if she had time and then she asked excitedly, 'Could we?'

'Of course we can, and I'll give you a quick tour of my new house.'

Shelley's face filled with excitement and she shouted, 'I'll race you there.' She pulled on the reins and turned her horse to face in the direction of the Henshall Ranch and heeled it into a gallop.

⋆   ⋆   ⋆

When the ranch-house appeared into view it reminded her of one of the stately homes she'd seen in drawings in a classical English novel.

Uncle Bryn was breathless and red in the face when he dismounted and helped Shelley down. She could smell the liquor on his breath and wondered if he had started celebrating her wedding already. Shelley stood and admired the fine entrance with its heavy oak door.

'You never did see inside, did you?' he asked.

'Remember we were all going to come over just before . . . ' Shelley didn't finish the sentence. The Morgan family visit had been arranged for the day after Lucy had been killed and Shelley didn't want to have sad thoughts today.

'Come on, I'll give you a five minute tour and then we'll go and get your present from the stables around the back.'

Shelley could see obvious signs of neglect when she entered the hallway and noticed the missing pictures on the walls beside the spiralling staircase. Uncle Bryn explained that Vincent had sold the pictures to help pay off some of his debts. The neglect couldn't detract from the magnificence of the surround-ings as they made their way up the giant staircase. There were no missing pictures on the top landing and she paused briefly as she admired the selection of paintings that were of horses, while Uncle Bryn explained that they were all of horses that had belonged to the Henshall family.

'You must see this room before you go,' he said as he pushed open the heavy door with its intricate carvings. Shelley followed him into the darkened room and he said he would open the shutters. A moment later the sunlight burst through the windows and she was able to see the large four-poster bed with the gold drapes hanging from it. She had begun to feel uneasy when she spotted the red rose on one of the pillows. She felt his breath on her neck and the strong smell of liquor reached her nostrils. She shuddered and felt more frightened than she had ever been in all her life.

'This can be our room, Shelley. You should have a room like this. You deserve more than the log cabin that Brannigan will have you slave away in.'

'Uncle Bryn, you're frightening me. I'm going now. You can bring me the foal some other time. Now I really must go.'

She was heading for the door, but stopped when he said, 'If you leave now, Shelley, I'll kill Brannigan.'

'Please don't say such things. Why are you being like this?' she pleaded.

'I don't want to hurt you, but if you don't give me the chance to talk to you, then I'll lock you in here and go and kill Brannigan. I'll never let you marry him. The truth is, Shelley, I've always loved you ever since you blossomed into the beautiful woman that you are now.'

'Please don't say these things, Uncle Bryn. Let's go home together and I promise that I will never tell anybody what you have just told me. I won't tell Pa, Mom, or even Carl. I swear that I will never tell a living soul.'

'I can't do that, Shelley. You've got to understand just how much I love you. I've even killed for you. I shot Daniel Jefferson this very morning to stop him pestering you and keeping me from talking with you. And that's why you'd better believe that I'll kill Brannigan unless you give him up. I've already tried to get rid of him once, but I'll succeed next time because I won't care if I get caught. I've decided that if I can't have you then my life won't be worth living. I would have shot him in the church today if you'd got that far.'

Shelley tried to calm herself and humour him when she said, 'But we could never be together because you're my uncle and it would be a sin.'

He smiled and said. 'But I'm not. I'm not your uncle and that's another secret you didn't know about. I was left on the Morgans' doorstep when I was a baby. Abandoned by my own mother. Maybe that's why I've hated women until now.'

Shelley started to run for the door and he seized her and began trying to kiss her. She squirmed and turned her face away.

'Maybe he won't want you if he finds

out that his little Miss Innocent is soiled.'

Shelley screamed as she realized his intentions and then she felt the full force of his hand when he slapped her across the face. He dragged her to the bed and pushed her on to it. She was dazed for a second, but struggled as he ripped her clothes. The sight of her naked breasts made him wild with desire. He struck her again, this time with his fist as she tried to raise herself off the bed. She lay motionless as he fumbled to remove his own clothing. He ripped the undergarment from her and then straddled her before forcing himself on her with a savagery driven by crazed passion.

She was barely conscious as he lay beside her, stroking her face, telling her how sorry he was, but claiming that it was for the best and that she would learn to love him. She groaned with pain as he went on. 'We'll sleep for a while, and then I'll go get you a drink and I'll bring some water to bathe your face. Why did you make me hurt you? But everything is going to be all right. We can tell everyone that I rescued you from being attacked by Daniel Jefferson and brought you here. In a few months' time we'll move to another town and get married. I've got all the money we'll ever need. We can live together like it was always meant to be. Until then it'll just be our little secret.'

She had fainted and didn't hear the rest of his plans.

* * *

When Shelley's senses cleared, she prayed that it had been a nightmare, but she knew it had been real. She ached all over. She could still smell the liquor from his breath. She kept still at first, fearing that she might awake him, but the room was silent and when she turned towards where he had been, he wasn't there. She knew he would be back.

She sobbed gently as she relived the

horror that had destroyed so much. There would be no wedding now, not to Carl and not to any man. Carl would have stood by her, she knew that, but she couldn't live with the shame. She also knew that she would not be her daddy's sweet girl ever again. She climbed slowly off the bed, determined that the monster who had tricked her would not get the chance to touch her again. The short walk to the window was painful and when she reached it she struggled to open it, finally succeeding and welcoming the cold air on her face.

She gasped with the pain as she climbed on to the window ledge. Her eyes stung with the salt from her tears and she couldn't make out who the approaching rider was. It must be him returning from a trip into town, but it didn't really matter who it was. She said a silent goodbye to her loved ones and jumped.

19

Carl had spent his second sleepless night since the day he and Shelley should have been married. On his way back to the ranch-house from the Collins place he had met up with WJ and told him what had happened. He'd asked him to go back to town and bring Mr Beaumont to collect Shelley's body. WJ was to make sure that Beaumont brought a funeral gown because Carl wanted to make sure that the Morgan family were spared the details of what had taken place while she was held captive in the ranch-house. It was Stanley Beaumont who had discovered that Shelley had been clutching the gentleman's small gold watch in her hand. It was engraved with Bryn Morgan's initials and contained a photograph of Shelley inside it.

Carl would never forget the moment

he broke the news to William and Kathryn Morgan. William Morgan said that he wondered why a family could have been inflicted with so much tragedy. He would grieve for his daughters until his dying day, but he hoped that his brother, Bryn, was rotting in hell. It was no surprise that they would be leaving Maple tomorrow. William Morgan said that he had asked his lawyer to transfer ownership of the Henshall Ranch over to Carl. They hoped that one day he would also rebuild his own ranch where their daughter had planned to spend the rest of her life. He told them of his plans to return to Bugle Falls and work as a lawman, but he intended to return one day and settle down. The Morgans hoped he would take a wife and be happy. He didn't tell them that he would never marry, or that he'd vowed to his Shelley as she lay in her coffin that she would live in his memory for-ever, and that no one would ever replace her. It was a vow he intended to keep.

WJ had made him a farewell breakfast and he'd done his best to eat it as so many thoughts raced through his mind. WJ made a final plea when he said, 'You know you're going to be missed around here, buddy, and Marshal Burrows told me again last night that he would stand down and let you take the marshal's job.'

'He's a good man and I appreciate the offer, but I need to get away. I'll be feeling raw for a long time and being around here wouldn't help. I'm going to miss you as well, buddy, and I hope you'll pay me a visit in Bugle Falls before too long.'

'I will, and don't you worry about the ranch. I'll make sure that no squatters move in. Anyway, I'd better get going and relieve the new deputy. I nearly forgot. Mr Beaumont called in the office yesterday and said that his assistants had gone out to the Collins place to pick up Bryn Morgan's body.

Mr Beaumont said they only found some large bones, but nothing that was worth burying. The marshal thinks the body must have been dragged away by some animals, probably wolves.'

'He didn't deserve a burial,' was all that Carl said. The two men shook hands and hugged. WJ had reached the door when Carl called after him, 'I never did thank you properly for saving my life the other night. You're one hell of a deputy.'

WJ gave him a thumbs up sign and hurried away to hide his awkwardness and sadness.

* * *

Carl had ridden up to the hill and was surveying the scene below. He had gone to the cemetery and visited the graves of his parents and little Lucy, the girl he had never known. He'd sat near Shelley's grave until he saw some people come into the cemetery. They were Daniel Jefferson's family. It seemed that Daniel hadn't any experience with girls and that's why he'd pestered Shelley, but he really had been harmless. His family would probably never be certain who had shot him dead near the trail that Shelley had taken, but Carl had no doubt that it had been Bryn Morgan.

He took a last look at the blazing Henshall ranch-house where he'd started the fire some two hours ago. He'd spent the most of yesterday filling the house with straw in preparation for today. He paused for a moment by the yew tree he had visited so often with Shelley and then heeled his horse forward to start his journey to Bugle Falls and a new life.

THE END

We do hope that you have enjoyed reading this large print book.

Did you know that all of our titles are available for purchase?

We publish a wide range of high quality large print books including:
Romances, Mysteries, Classics
General Fiction
Non Fiction and Westerns

Special interest titles available in large print are:
The Little Oxford Dictionary
Music Book, Song Book
Hymn Book, Service Book

Also available from us courtesy of Oxford University Press:
Young Readers' Dictionary
(large print edition)
Young Readers' Thesaurus
(large print edition)

For further information or a free brochure, please contact us at:
Ulverscroft Large Print Books Ltd.,
The Green, Bradgate Road, Anstey,
Leicester, LE7 7FU, England.
Tel: (00 44) **0116 236 4325**
Fax: (00 44) **0116 234 0205**